Merridy has always loved music but can't sing. The only job in the music business he can get is as a security guard for the Bard and Sons, a premier record label. He keeps their secrets and patrols their hallways, always wishing for a big break he knows will never come.

Changeling's Court is a brand new band struggling to record their first single. Merridy chances upon a scrap of their lyrics without accompanying music notes and can't help composing a simple melody for them. If he's found out, he'll probably get fired.

Instead, he finds himself in a strange new world of magic and faeries—and danger.

I0591332

IF A BUTTERFLY DON'T FLY

Out of Underhill, Book Two

Mell Eight

A NineStar Press Publication

www.ninestarpress.com

If A Butterfly Don't Fly

Printed in the USA

ISBN: 978-1-64890-244-4

First Edition, April, 2021

Also available in eBook, ISBN: 978-1-64890-243-7

A Promise and a Warning

Composed By: Unknown

Faery dust and the rolling greens,
A life of love, a love of thrills,
We the people from under the hills
Offer the sweetest of dreams.

Ware, you be and you will live
For the wee folk take all.
Then laugh, happy as you fall,
And our pains we never forgive.

Of underhill and overstone,
Lakes and rivers that always flow,
Skies above and the caverns below,
The faery court rules by blood and bone.

Faery dust and the rolling greens,
Devious, cruel, and oh so sweet,
You should hope we never do meet
Above, below, and always unseen.

Tell me, how good is your luck tonight?

Chapter One

Music was embedded in the very fibers of the building.

Merridy took a deep breath as he stepped out of the stairwell and onto the first floor of practice rooms and felt the remnants of the notes played on instruments and sung into microphones swirling around him. They chimed in his ears and seemed to fill the air with a shine he could almost reach out and touch. Merridy wanted to touch it so badly, but instead, he let out his breath and smoothed down the front of his security guard uniform before reaching for the door handle that led into the first private lounge, which belonged to a soloist named Amaryllis.

As he stepped inside, Merridy saw Amaryllis's bra hanging from the back of a chair. It was lacy across the tops of the cups, the sort of bra that, if the front of her shirt slipped while she was sweaty from singing onstage under the hot lights, might look like a fancy camisole peeking through.

Normally, Merridy didn't mind the overnight shift as a security guard at the headquarters of the Bard and Sons. There wasn't anyone else around as he walked through the halls half lit by security lighting and the ambient light that filtered in through the windows from the parking lot outside. He enjoyed the quiet and the solitude—and the music. He couldn't sing any of the notes aloud, of course, but he could hear each note in his head as if the musicians were still hard at work. Sometimes he took the notes he heard and wrote them down; he had notebooks full of songs he'd heard, of notes that had twined through his mind, all put down onto the bar lines preprinted on staff paper and filed on his bookshelves at home.

He wasn't used to running into women's underwear, though. Today, all he had expected coming in was the rather minor suspense of the new band taking over the lone empty practice room. Any sort of excitement to break up the monotony of walking in circles all night was a relief, and finding out what type of band—pop, rock, country—had moved in would be the highlight of his evening. He wanted to know what the remnants of their music would sound like when he stepped into their empty practice lounge, and if it was as good as he hoped, he was looking forward to buying their soundtrack to hear it firsthand.

Of course, what he really wanted was to be playing in his own band in the light of day, rather than sneaking hints of the sounds of other bands as he walked through each room at night, but he was taking what little he could get and trying to enjoy it as best he could.

He quickly checked the rest of the room to make sure it was completely empty, which included looking behind doors and inside the full wardrobe. Merridy closed the wardrobe doors, took one more look around the cluttered lounge, and hurried back into the hallway.

Merridy unhooked his keys from his belt and made sure the lounge door was firmly locked. Then he reached into his pocket and pulled out a small pad of organizer tabs, the ones usually used to keep school notes organized. He chose a red tab and yanked it free of the roll before sticking it to the underside of Amaryllis's nameplate. It would warn anyone arriving in the morning that this door should remain closed and locked until Amaryllis herself came to clean up her mess. Not even the morning custodian was allowed to go in to vacuum.

A bra was fairly innocuous, but given who it belonged to, it would probably sell for big bucks online. Merridy's simple red tab would keep anyone stupid enough to try— like the sound mixer who had been selling used drumsticks on eBay a few months back—from having the opportunity.

With Amaryllis's room done, Merridy continued down the hallway to the next door. It opened to reveal one of the two recording studios on the floor. He wasn't allowed to touch any of the electrical parts, like the blinking lights or the slides on the sound mixer board. He didn't know what any of the buttons did, and if he inadvertently ruined a project left unfinished overnight, he would be in major trouble.

He walked past the electronics and into the inner studio, where the instruments and the microphones for the singers were located. He could almost hear what the room sounded like when the instruments were playing— guitars riffing, drums pounding, and the simple note of a piano or bass holding it all together. The melodies would soar, reverberating through the room as a singer crooned into the mesh-fronted mic stand. Merridy knew what that sounded like from the dozens of auditions he had tried out for, and he'd reveled in each and every experience, but it didn't matter how good he was on keys or strings. Once the band found out he couldn't sing, somehow he was never actually chosen.

The imagined music faded from Merridy's thoughts as that harsh dose of reality set in. He quickly checked that the inner studio was also empty of people and continued on. He left the studio door as he'd found it: unlocked and tab-free. There wasn't anything sensitive to hide there.

Merridy checked behind every door—including the janitor's closet—for trespassers. Very famous, platinum-selling artists used the studio space or kept practice lounges in the building. Rabid fans and competitors alike would kill and bribe for even the slightest glimpse of what Merridy saw every night. Some things Merridy wished he could unsee. Stars were very strange people, and he didn't envy the custodians who had to clean up after them.

He finished his round of the floor where he had originally started, at the lone staircase in the corner. There was an elevator on the other side, but Merridy had to take the stairs up to the second floor first to ensure they were clear. He input his code into the keypad on the door to tell the other security guard manning the phones and desk in the lobby downstairs that he had finished the floor before heading farther upstairs.

The next two floors were comprised of more studio space. He had to flag one room on the third floor where someone had left a bong and some weed lying on a table next to a guitar.

He headed to the fourth floor, which was an exact replica of the prior two. Merridy walked to the first doorway and popped it open with a grimace. Soul Sound was a hard-rocking, hard-partying band, and their practice studio still sounded like it. The music floating through the air was a little shrieky, with high-pitched runs of the guitar accompanied by deep-throated screaming into the microphone. There were plenty of people who liked screamer rock, but Merridy just couldn't find enough of the melody floating through his mind to enjoy it himself. He tried not to listen for as long as he could manage while he flipped open doors and checked behind furniture.

The job of a security guard was boring and monotonous, and often weird. This first walkthrough of all the rooms was the most interesting part of his night, because he never knew just what he would find behind each closed door. After the surprise was gone, the hours slowly trickled by until the sun rose. The daytime security guards, who only had to sit at the desk in the lobby unless an issue occurred upstairs, would arrive, and Merridy could go home to sleep.

He swept all the rooms on the floor like usual, luckily not seeing anything too startling, until he reached the final door. The nameplate he was used to was gone, and the blank rectangle of wall where it used to be was slightly darker than the paint around it. It had been carefully removed; the holes for the screws didn't look torn or destroyed. Merridy turned and opened the studio door.

The furniture was different, too, as were the instruments scattered across the room. Antiquities and Wine—the country band that the space belonged to—had needed banjo stands, but those were now replaced by an upright piano. A leather jacket, another thing that didn't fit with Antiquities and Wine's chosen image, had been carelessly left across the back of the new couch.

Antiquities and Wine had moved to new studio space recently built farther south, Merridy remembered suddenly. That tidbit of information had gone out in the company's weekly internal email bulletin. A new band had already taken the space. Merridy wondered who they were. The space felt quiet, almost anticipatory, as the old notes in the air faded without Antiquities and Wine there to renew them. The new band hadn't yet begun to fill the space with their own sound.

He walked farther into the room, seeing four guitars—a bass, two electric, and one acoustic—on stands and a drum snare on top of the new piano. They were probably a pop-rock or rock band. In the back of the room, near the private bathroom, was a desk strewn with staff paper. Many of the sheets had been crumpled into balls and tossed aside. The ones still flat on the desk had dozens of cross-outs, some lines excessively crossed, the pen having cut deep.

Songwriting obviously wasn't going too well for the new band.

Well. Either they'd figure it out, or they'd get out. That was the way the business worked. They had been given their chance with the nice studio. If the band blew it, too bad. It was more of a chance than Merridy had ever had. He sighed and resolutely pushed his jealousy away before heading into the bathroom to double-check it was empty. Merridy had a good job. Just because he wanted to switch places with someone in the new band wasn't reason enough to let resentment simmer and ruin his night. The sink, toilet, and glassed-in shower stall hid no one, so he turned to head back out.

There was one piece of regular lined paper on the desk next to the bathroom door that wasn't crumpled or covered in pencil scratches. Merridy couldn't help stopping to read the four simple lines handwritten there.

In my dreams, I know you see me,

And in my hopes, you'll hold my hand.

Reality hits, so does the truth:

You and me will never be we.

It was the start of a song—the first stanza. A love song, maybe, or about a heartbreak. It had potential to be either, but only if the band could turn the detritus of staff paper into workable notes.

It wasn't any of Merridy's business whether they could or not.

He left the room, closing and locking the door behind him. Merridy pulled out a yellow tab and stuck it where the nameplate used to be. The barely composed verse wasn't really enough reason to mark the door as containing something sensitive, but it was close enough. The next three floors in the building were cubicle farms where the administrative sections of the Bard and Sons worked, and checking under desks and in the bathrooms was a quick job.

Merridy was walking the seventh floor—private offices he had to check individually—when he realized he was soundlessly humming a gentle lullaby tune to himself. The notes were original, vibrating inside his head one by one.

He stopped walking as words appeared in his mind's eye, slowly twining with the chiming notes and gently pulsing beat as the lullaby grew into a ballad in his head. *In my dreams, I know you see me.* Simple notes, none of the five-note chords Merridy had seen heavily crossed out in the new band's room. His version would show off the range of the singer's voice and the purity of it without overuse of accompanying instruments.

His fingers twitched, wanting the feel of the hard, ivory keys of a piano or the stiff strings of a guitar beneath them. He couldn't sing the notes, but he could play them. His mother had made sure of that early on.

He was just like his father, she always insisted. Even today, when he was twenty-five and out of the house, he would do something, and she would tut and smile and reference his father. She had only spent two months with the man as a groupie, living the dream on his father's sold-out nationwide tour. The Tuatha Dé Danann—the Goddess's Children, in English—had been one of the greatest rock bands of the time, and his mother one of their most fervent fans.

His father had played guitar for Tuatha Dé Danann and couldn't speak a word. Merridy had seen pictures of him from those days, before the band had vanished into the nameless ether that was real life. He and his father could have been twins, if not for the age difference. They had the same cherry-red hair and green eyes, rounded cheekbones, full lips, and pert nose. Merridy was short like his mother, but otherwise, she said he was his father's through and through.

Merridy shook his head violently, trying to get the melancholy thoughts and the tune out. He was on the clock and couldn't be caught dawdling. This job was the closest he had ever come to the music industry, and he wasn't about to blow it with what-ifs and hopeless dreams. He kept walking, checking each office as he went.

So what if he had wanted to follow in his father's footsteps and play guitar or piano for a famous band? When they found out he couldn't sing at auditions, he went nowhere. His father had been mute, too, but there was no way to know what extra ability his dad had that Merridy was missing that had allowed him to soar while Merridy remained stuck. A security guard was a perfectly fine job, and it was even better that he got to work for the Bard and Sons. He could pretend he was waiting for his big break, instead of wallowing at the only job he could get in the business.

The final floor was for the bigwigs. Men and women with director, CEO, and talent manager attached to their names held court in the gigantic and fancy offices Merridy walked through. This was the quickest floor because it had the fewest desks to check. In fact, the only space with even a little clutter was the massive office assistant's desk in the miniature lobby in front of the elevator. Merridy looped through the floor, then headed back to the elevator.

The elevator doors opened smoothly a few seconds later. Merridy stepped inside, swiped his badge through the scanner, and hit the button for the first-floor lobby. The elevator was clear, too, with no signs of tampering to the electrical panel or the roof hatch. The elevator dinged and the doors slid open again, revealing the fancy marble and glass lobby with the receptionists' and security guards' desks. At night, Stan was the only person there to watch the cameras and to let anyone using the building late in and out.

"Any problems, kid?" Stan asked. He put aside the night's crossword as Merridy rounded the security desk, smiling enough to show off the burgeoning crow's feet and laugh lines crinkling his dark face. His only duties were to watch the door and the monitors for the cameras outside, answer the phone, and check on Merridy's progress as he got to each keypad, and he did his job well, for all that he spent most of his energy on his puzzles.

Merridy shook his head.

"All right then," Stan grunted. "Head on back. I'll give you a holler when it's time to make another round."

Merridy nodded, waving his hand in thanks. A small lamp and a half-dozen miniature TVs showing blinking camera feeds lit Stan's crossword as Merridy slipped behind his chair and through the door there. Stan had everything under control.

The security room had industrial-sized lockers to the right and a small locked munitions and supplies cage to the left. In the middle was a utilitarian kitchen table. Merridy's book and a bottle of water were right where he had left them before his shift had started. He settled into one of the uncomfortable chairs around the table, drank some water, and opened his book. Then he stared uncomprehendingly at the words for fifteen minutes while the ballad again took form in his head.

Simple notes and a slow beat that gave plenty of time for the words to form and soar. Merridy could almost see each individual note fluttering through the air, twining with the lyrics like a cat around his ankles. *And in my hopes, you'll hold my hand.* Breathy, but still strong.

"Kid, time to go!" Stan banged on the door with one fist, and Merridy jumped. He closed his book and ran a hand through his hair, wondering what was wrong with him that he couldn't relax after walking nearly two miles of building. If he didn't take time to unwind, his legs would feel like wet noodles by the end of the night. He knew that, yet the melody continued to harass him even as he waved at Stan and headed for the staircase again.

His second round of the night was completely uneventful until he reached the new band's practice room again. He couldn't help hesitating at the desk, staring down at the words and thinking about the music in his head. He resolutely moved away but only got as far as the piano.

He hit middle C and frowned because that wasn't right. Then he hit E, paused to study the keys, and hit B. B wasn't quite right either, so he tapped B flat, and the melody in his head soared.

Merridy fled the room and continued on his rounds.

He waved an all clear to Stan when he stepped out of the elevator and returned to his seat in the back for another fifteen minutes of rest. Technically he was only supposed to get two forty-five-minute breaks during his six-hour shift, but cutting it up into fifteen-minute chunks every hour worked better for him.

Not that he was getting any real rest in between rounds. The B flat was an interesting touch, a bit of dissonance to emphasize the bitter feelings the words evoked. It wouldn't work all the time, not as a full chord, but a touch of it here and there would give the song impact.

On his fifth round, he picked up a piece of blank treble staff paper off the desk, neatly folded it up, and stuck it in his pocket. On his way past Stan once his round was over, he grabbed one of the extra pencils Stan always had lying around and hurried to the table in the back room. It took him all fifteen minutes to write the notes down. It was hard to get the time signature correct, and the right number of notes for each measure, but he was just filling in the circle of the final quarter note when Stan yelled out.

Merridy tucked the paper into his pocket and got back to work.

"Last one of the night, kid," Stan said as Merridy joined him in the lobby. Merridy grinned and nodded, already looking forward to the drive home. He put both of his palms together and tucked them under one cheek as he made heavy breathing noises. "Oh, yeah. Sleep sounds nice right about now," Stan laughed. "You read my number right."

He waved Merridy off, and Merridy hurried to the stairs. His head was finally free of the melody, but the staff paper was burning a hole in his pocket. He needed to drop it off and forget about it. Ten to one, the band would probably think it was another of their scratched and discarded sheets and toss it. Still, Merridy couldn't help gently placing the paper down next to the one where the stanza was written.

He hurried away, moving on to the next floor and vowing to forget about it entirely.

When the elevator dropped him back in the lobby, sunlight was quickly replacing the street lighting through the windows, and the overhead electric lights on a timer were beginning to click on. The two members of the six a.m. to noon shift, Brice and Jimmy, were already taking their places behind the security desk, where they would stay unless something happened.

Merridy waved and gave the all-clear signal.

"You're dismissed, then," Brice said sharply, her booming voice cutting through the otherwise silent lobby. The first of the receptionists would be arriving in the next hour, but Merridy would be long gone by then.

Merridy nodded and hurried into the locker room. He changed out of his uniform, tossing the pants and shirt into the laundry pile and hanging his hat and belt in his locker. He put on his own clothes, grabbed his things, and left. He waved to Brice as he slipped around the desk and headed out the front doors that had just been unlocked for normal business hours.

Merridy walked out to where his car was waiting, parked in its designated spot. He had to pause halfway through backing out to let out a wide, jaw-cracking yawn. It was definitely bedtime.

At six a.m., the streets were just starting to perk up with morning rush hour traffic. Most drivers were heading out of the suburbs—in the opposite direction Merridy was traveling—so there were almost no cars in his lane.

His thoughts were filled with the last two hardboiled eggs in his fridge and some instant oatmeal when flashing lights in his rearview mirror caught his attention. The blue-and-red strobes were on his car's tail. Merridy pulled over, hoping the police car just needed to get past him, but his heart sank when the cruiser stopped behind him instead.

He hadn't been speeding, so maybe this was just a random stop. There had been a problem with a few kids stealing their parents' cars to go joyriding in the past; maybe the officer thought Merridy looked too young to be behind the wheel. He was twenty-five, but his mom insisted he barely looked eighteen. He dug out his wallet for his license and popped open the glove compartment to grab his registration. He also got out his emergency pad of paper and a pen, because the chances of the officer knowing sign language were slim.

Finally, the officer got out of his car and strolled over to Merridy's.

"License and registration," the cop barked, not even noticing that Merridy was already holding them out through the rolled-down car window. The officer snatched both from Merridy's hand, almost violently, and stomped back to his car.

Something wasn't right. Merridy had been pulled over before, and the officer always asked about the crime committed first. "Do you know how fast you were going?" or "Did you see that stop sign back there?" Traffic officers in particular liked to be as genial as possible in order to avoid getting run over by the people they were stopping.

Merridy noted the cruiser's license plate number and car number. He wrote both down, as well as the date and time, on a blank page in his emergency notebook. He also wrote down a quick description of the officer: in uniform, brown hair, tall, heavily muscled.

When he saw the cruiser door open again, Merridy flipped back a few pages to one covered with other writing and found a blank space to write, "May I please see your badge, Officer?"

He took his paperwork back from the officer and pointed to his question. The officer bent forward slightly to read it, then grunted and reached into his pocket. The badge he pulled out looked official, not that Merridy could spot a fake, and he tucked it away almost as fast as he had pulled it out. Still, Merridy had managed to get a good look at what the badge had said. Badge number 9356, Officer Hadley James. Merridy did his best to memorize it until he could flip back a page and write it down.

"This ticket can still be voided," Officer James said suddenly, holding out the long piece of paper his cruiser's computer had spat out.

Merridy tilted his head as if he were asking "how" and waited for Officer James to continue speaking.

"You just need to answer one question for me, and this can all go away. We can pretend it never happened," James continued, his eyes sharp and piercing as if his formidable gaze could force Merridy into answering. "Tell me about the new band the Bard and Sons just signed."

Merridy managed to keep his face blank. The internal memo he only half remembered hadn't given any information that he could think of, just that a new band would be occupying the space vacated by Antiquities and Wine. Still, even if Merridy had known, he wouldn't tell anyone.

He drew a large question mark on his paper and shrugged.

"Fine," Officer James snapped again. He thrust the ticket at Merridy, turned around with a snort of disgust, and headed back to his car. The cruiser pulled away from the curb before Merridy had even started his own car again, which was definitely against police procedure, and vanished back toward the shopping strip. When the car was out of sight, Merridy flipped back through his pad of paper and wrote down everything, from badge number and name to exactly what had been said. The ticket was for failing to signal a turn, something so mundane in a world of reckless speeders that it was almost laughable. Merridy put his car back in drive and headed home.

Eating breakfast wasn't nearly as important to Merridy now. He parked his car in the garage of his little ranch-style house and hurried inside. His laptop was charging in the bedroom. He popped the top open and waited for the wireless internet to connect before opening a new email window.

The cop could have been a bribery attempt by a competitor music company, but it could also just as easily be a test by his employer. Either way, Merridy didn't want to lose his job over something so silly. He quickly typed up everything he had written down and anything else he could think of before sending the email to his supervisor, Sarika. He paced around his bedroom for a few long minutes, waiting for a reply.

He needed to do laundry, if the piles of dirty clothes he was skirting were any indication. Instead of spending more time pacing, Merridy gathered some clothes together and headed across the house to the kitchen where the laundry machines were tucked away near the garage door. He started a load before stopping at the fridge for his eggs and some juice. He didn't have the patience to deal with oatmeal at the moment.

An email was waiting for him when he returned to his computer.

Thank you for telling us about this, Sarika had written. *We'll look into the incident at once. Don't worry about the traffic ticket. We'll take care of it for you.*

Just like that, exhaustion hit him like a brick. After a long night of work and dealing with the morning's mess, he was ready to fall into bed and sleep straight through until his next shift. Never mind the errands or finishing the laundry. Never mind the worry over the ticket and the music notes he had left for the band. Sleep sounded so much better than allowing stomach-churning anxiety to take hold.

He stuffed the last bit of egg in his mouth and got undressed while he was chewing. Merridy climbed into bed in just his boxers, pulled the covers over his head, and resolutely drifted off to sleep.

Chapter Two

Merridy parked his car in the lot at the Bard and Sons at ten minutes to midnight. He killed the engine and then just sat in the car for a few seconds. He had to take deep breaths to calm himself.

He didn't know what he would find when he walked into work. Sarika had said the traffic ticket had been taken care of, but what if something more had happened during the day? Had the new band noticed the notes he had written for them? What if they hadn't? Or, worse, what if they had? What would Merridy do?

Minutes ticked away on his dashboard clock. If he was late to work on top of everything else, he really would be in trouble. He took one last breath before resolutely opening the car door and stepping outside into the cool autumn night.

The front doors of the building were still unlocked. They would automatically lock at exactly 12:01, and Stan would have to physically unlock them to let anyone working overtime out of the building.

Liv was sitting at the security desk, her arms crossed as she studied the cameras. The last receptionist was shutting down her computer. "Sarika left a note for you,"

Liv said amicably as he drew even with her. Their lives only overlapped for the short minutes while Merridy was changing into his uniform and she was waiting for Stan to take over her post. "One of the bigwigs is still in his office, top floor."

Merridy nodded as he walked to the door behind the desk. Stan was just tightening his belt on his uniform when Merridy walked into the locker room. He waved hello in reply to Stan's absentminded grunt and headed to his own locker to get dressed.

Nothing changed when one of the bosses was still at work and Merridy had to patrol. He just had to act polite and discreet should they see him, but he wasn't to go out of his way to avoid or approach them.

Sarika's note was taped to his locker. It was a simple, folded piece of lined paper with his name on the outside. Merridy yanked the note down and opened it to find Sarika's tight script written inside.

> *Traffic ticket is taken care of. Don't take any further action with it. The police officer is under internal investigation.*

Merridy rolled his eyes and crumpled up the note, glad to let that one worry go. He lobbed it into a nearby trashcan before turning to unlock his locker and dig out his uniform.

Liv and the receptionist were gone by the time Merridy had finished getting changed and headed out to the security desk. Aside from the boss working late upstairs, it was shaping up to be a normal night. Even the boss being around wasn't too unusual, really. Merridy waved again at Stan and then headed to the staircase to start his first round of the night.

The first floor was unremarkable, as were the next two floors up. One of the bands had left some porn magazines open on a table in their lounge. Merridy figured the custodian would get a good laugh out of *Big Jugs Do Vegas* before he realized the disgusting mess he had to clean. It wasn't enough to force Merridy to lock the door, but Merridy did make a mental note to walk the far way around the couch on his next round.

At the end of the fourth floor was the room Merridy was both dreading and anticipating. A nameplate still hadn't been added to the wall next to the door. From the outside, the room almost looked unoccupied. A couple of artists had decorated their doors with band stickers, but the new group hadn't touched the outside of theirs.

Despite his reluctance to see how his notes had been received, Merridy still had a job to do. He reached out, trying to ignore the fact that his hand was shaking slightly and his heart had suddenly ratcheted up its pounding, and opened the door.

The room was empty, which he should have expected, but he still let out an involuntary gasp of air. There was music all around him, the deep thrum of the bass guitar and the simple hum of piano keys whose notes were held to allow a full-bodied harmony. Merridy also sensed a touch of discord, as if the music wasn't quite flowing smoothly from fingers to instruments.

Merridy realized he was standing, frozen, in the doorway, and forced himself to step into the room. He did his check quickly, looking behind chairs and inside cabinets, all the while trying to ignore the enticing music. After a few short moments, all that was left to check was the bathroom. And the table he had to walk past to get there.

He couldn't look at the table on his way into the bathroom. Out of the corner of his eye, he saw that it was still as cluttered as ever, but he forced himself to walk by without turning his head. The bathroom was empty. Merridy double-checked the shower twice and even looked in the tiny cabinet under the sink. He was just stalling, he knew that. But at the same time, he couldn't help it. Eventually, he had no choice but to move on.

He stepped slowly out of the bathroom and just as slowly turned his head to look at the table. The balled-up pieces of paper had been moved around, and new, scratched-out staff lines of music notes had replaced some of the old. In the very center of the table was one single piece of neat staff paper. The stanza of lyrics from the night before had been written there, along with what looked like a second stanza. The notes Merridy had written were also on the paper, carefully handwritten into the correct places on the staff.

Harmony had been added for a second voice. The notes rang through Merridy's head as he read them. The harmonies spiraled, and the purposeful dissonance Merridy had included was subtly emphasized along with the lyrics.

An expert at the art of crafting music had taken the small ballad Merridy had left and woven it into something magical.

In my dreams, I know you see me,
And in my hopes, you'll hold my hand.
Reality hits, so does the truth:
You and me will never be we.

Another dream, a hand on my shoulder,
Someone smiling only at me.
You're laughing, so happy.
Reality hits, and I'm still alone.

Merridy reached the bottom of the page with a start. The music ended abruptly, clearly unfinished. He couldn't help reaching out to pick up the page, looking for more. There was a second page, but it didn't have notes—just another stanza of lyrics.

If a butterfly don't fly, it falls.
You are my wings; you are my wings,
Broken wings, shattered, torn.
You are my wings, and I'm falling hard.

It felt almost like a chorus, and the three scant half notes penciled onto the paper emphasized that feeling. They were in the same key as the rest of the song, but the timing and the chord progression had changed. It was unfinished and very promising. Merridy could hear how the chorus could continue, with emphasis for the range of the singer's voice with a falsetto run of sixteenth notes. He could end it on a dark note to coincide with the negative lyrics, all while still tying the chorus to the potential of another stanza. It would be so easy to pick up a pencil and write down the notes.

Instead, Merridy replaced the top page and spun away from the table. His legs were shaking slightly from the effort it took, but he walked away. He had rounds to complete, and he had already spent enough time going through papers he had no business touching. Besides, it looked like they didn't need his help. Only a master musician could have put together something so complex from the little bit Merridy had written down the previous night. The band probably hadn't needed Merridy's input in the first place, and since the chorus was already started, they might resent Merridy's continued interference.

He tapped his code into the waiting keypad and jogged up the stairs, hoping the extra physical effort might jar the song loose from inside his head. He was also running a bit late, so he speed-walked through the administration floors—still making sure to be thorough as he checked each cubicle—and by the time he reached the top floor, he was back to his usual timing. Good thing, too, because when he stepped onto the floor and saw light shining out of one office, he remembered there was a high-level executive in the company working late, so he had to act dignified instead of rushed and panicked.

Merridy still couldn't get the song out of his head. The harmonies from the first part flowed straight into the chorus that he didn't dare write down. He was walking in exact time with the song too, Merridy realized when his foot paused briefly in the air at the exact place a rest had been written into the music. He needed to focus on his job, on the executive, and not on the song. Merridy took a deep breath and concentrated. He could do this.

The lit office belonged to Boyd Rylee, the Artist and Repertoire Director. Merridy had never met him, but Director Rylee looked up and nodded politely as Merridy walked by.

Stan looked at him briefly as the elevator doors slid open. Merridy nodded an all clear and Stan returned to his crosswords. Merridy sank into one of the chairs in the break room. He tried to clear his mind and banish the music. He had never been able to do it before, and he didn't know why he thought he could now. Music was in his soul, and it had a song it wanted to get out.

There was only one solution, Merridy realized as the dissonance played through his head again before soaring off into the harmony of the chorus. He had to write the notes of the chorus. He didn't need to leave it for the band. Instead, he could take it home and tuck it away where no one would ever find it, and hopefully the music would let him be for a while. No other band had ever affected him like this. It wasn't the first time he had seen lyrics or notes left scattered around the studio, yet for some reason this band—this song—kept tiptoeing note by note across his brain.

Merridy jumped, surprised, when Stan pounded on the door.

"Time to go, kid!" he yelled. Fifteen minutes had whizzed by without Merridy realizing it. He screwed the cap back on his water and headed out to do his next round. He had to steady himself before he pushed open the door to the new band's practice room. He checked it thoroughly, and on his way past the table he slipped a piece of blank staff paper into one pocket.

The round ended with the usual ding as the elevator doors opened to let Merridy off in the lobby.

"Back again, kid," Stan stated with a shrug. "What's that bigwig doing up there? Sitting at his oversized desk, looking important?" He snorted in disgust. Merridy shrugged, unsure how to answer that. He had no idea what Director Rylee was doing while working so late. "Of course he is," Stan sighed. "He gets paid the big bucks to look important while you and me wallow with an hourly salary."

Merridy shrugged again to answer Stan's complaining. Luckily, Stan had never bothered to learn any sign language, so Merridy didn't have to think up an actual answer.

"Well, whatever," Stan grumped. "Go have your break."

In the back room, Merridy pulled the staff paper out of his pocket and gently unfolded it. He found a pencil and started drawing musical notes. His hand was shaking slightly, but the melody in his head was strong and clear.

Writing music was exactly like writing in a foreign language. Each note had a specific place to go on the lines of the staff. Its placement meant that the note made exactly one sound. The shape of the note told how many beats it was. In some ways, it was more complex than English. An A in English made a sound, which could then be combined with other letters to make words. It was exactly the same with an A in musical notes. That A could be twined with other notes to make sounds too.

Merridy could hear each note as it interacted with the rest of the song and the lyrics as he colored in the half notes. He wrote the lyrics in, too, to double-check that the beats in the music matched the syllables in the words. *If a butterfly don't fly, it falls.* That line in particular kept ringing in his head. He wanted to fly, too, with the strum of guitar strings under his fingers, the tap of piano keys, and the music buoying him into the air on wings of soaring harmonies. He did the best he could on his own, but without someone to play with—without someone to actually sing each of his notes aloud—he just couldn't fly.

The best way to tell if a song would sell millions of copies was the sheer emotion the lyrics and notes evoked. Just judging by the lyrics, Merridy knew this song would be a chart-topper.

"Time to go, kid!" Stan yelled through the door.

Merridy wasn't entirely satisfied with the last few notes, so he left the staff paper and his pencil on the table. It wasn't as if he was going to share it with anyone, but he just couldn't put it away without finishing it.

Stan was putting away his crossword book and straightening his uniform when Merridy joined him in the lobby.

"Looks like the bigwig is done for the night," he explained with a shrug toward the elevator. The floor numbers shown on a fancy electronic screen on top of the elevator were slowly rising as the elevator headed to the top floor. Stan checked the keys on his belt—he would need them ready to unlock the front doors to let Director Rylee out—and patted his cheeks so he would look a little more alert. "You head on upstairs for your rounds. No sense in you being late just to accommodate Mr. Hard Worker."

Merridy gave Stan a small smile to show he appreciated it. He headed to the stairs as the numbers on the elevator began to count down again. The inevitable keypads and the dozens of empty hallways and rooms awaited him.

Stan was buried in his crossword when Merridy returned to the lobby. He looked up perfunctorily as Merridy stepped out of the elevator. Merridy shrugged an all clear and headed into the break room.

Merridy thought he only needed to add one note to the end of the chorus. He wanted to include a touch of the harmony that had been woven for the first part of the song. It would be a good connection to the next verse.

Except the staff paper wasn't on the table.

Merridy gasped, staring in shock at the pencil sitting next to his bottle of water and the completely blank space on the table where the paper ought to be. Where could his music have gone? He checked under the table to see if it had blown off when the door opened, and then in the trash can in case Stan had thrown it away, thinking he was being helpful. It wasn't there either.

Panic started to overcome reason as Merridy checked underneath the lockers. Had Stan taken it? Had Merridy put it in his pocket accidentally and it was now lost somewhere only a custodian would find in the morning?

He looked everywhere, including inside his own locker and in Stan's. All Stan had in his locker was a change of clothes, a half-dozen more crossword books, and a handful of sharpened pencils. By the time Stan yelled and banged on the door, Merridy's only conclusion was that the paper was gone. He didn't know how it had vanished, but it was nowhere to be found.

He straightened his uniform hat on his head and took a few deep breaths to try to calm his heart rate and slow his racing thoughts. It wasn't as if he had been planning to share that music with anyone, so it didn't really matter that in thirty years when the company remodeled the security room and tore out the lockers, they would find the old and crumpled piece of staff paper. He had written down the song, had gotten it out of his head, and now he could relax and return to work without worrying about it.

"You okay in there?" Stan asked as Merridy walked out of the break room and stopped at his side to check in.

Merridy pulled over the slip of notepaper Stan kept on his desk for when they needed to communicate beyond nods and wrote: *dropped my bookmark and had to dig it out from under the lockers.*

"Man, that sucks," Stan said with a grimace. "Well, let's move the night along. I'll see you in a few." He returned to his crosswords, and Merridy headed to the staircase to start his next round.

*

Merridy woke up when his laptop started chiming at him from where it was perched on his nightstand. He huffed out a breath and rolled over, tangling his blankets around his feet in the process, to look at the clock. It was two o'clock in the afternoon, which was about two hours sooner than he would have liked to wake up.

The laptop let out another insistent chime—his video call ringtone. Since the only person who regularly called him was his mother, Merridy sighed and rolled back over until he could reach his laptop, pull it into his lap, and hit the green Connect button.

"Are you still in bed at this hour?" his mother immediately exclaimed after the call connected and the video turned on. Merridy was in his pajamas, a loose-fitting shirt over a pair of boxers. He had little doubt his hair was also in disarray.

"I was working late last night," he signed.

"Oh, that's right. I forgot," Mom sighed. She tucked a strand of hair behind an ear, her slight frown still unabated. Merridy had her lack of height, but otherwise he didn't look anything like her. Her hair was gray-shot blonde, curled to fall in waves to her shoulders, and her eyes were brown. "When are you going to get a job with real hours? I know the one you have pays really well, but a mother likes to take her son out for dinner sometimes."

"I'm available for dinner," he signed back. "I don't start work until midnight."

"Oh, bah. You know what I mean. Anyway"—she hurried to change the subject—"it's been a while since we chatted. Tell me what's going on with your life."

"Like what?" he asked with a sigh. Some things never changed. He should have hung up on her and gotten more sleep instead.

"Like...are you alone in bed right now, or is there a boy you should be introducing me to?"

"Mom!" Merridy signed, his fingers chopping out the normally elegant motion as his mouth fell open in shock.

"Well, is there?"

"No!"

She blew air out through her mouth, her lips flapping together in a fart sound. "Well, damn. I can't get any grandkids if you don't find a nice boy to marry." Merridy would have groaned if he had the voice to. He'd lost count of the times she had brought up the grandkids complaint. He did roll his eyes, but he made sure to do it when his mom wasn't looking. "Have you at least gone on a date recently?"

She looked so hopeful it almost physically hurt when he shook his head. How could he go on a date when he was always watching the clock so he wouldn't be late to work? Dinner and then a roll in the sheets—if he had been dating the guy he was with for a while—followed by Merridy jumping out of bed immediately afterward to shower and drive off. It didn't exactly express his confidence in the guy he was always leaving behind. The men and their hurt egos eventually got tired of it and left, which was why Merridy didn't bother going on dates anymore.

His mother let out another loud sigh and was just pulling in breath for what Merridy knew would be an awful tirade about how he wasn't even trying when his phone rang. The screen on his computer flashed to tell him he had a call waiting.

"I have to take this," Merridy signed before he had even looked at the number on the caller ID. It could have been the world's worst telemarketer, and he still would have told her that; he loved her, but her tirades were endless and exhausting.

"Fine," she grumbled, "but don't think you've escaped me. I'll call in a few days, and I hope you'll have different news to tell me!"

She hung up. Merridy took a deep breath before accepting the new call. Instead of a call connecting, a text message popped up.

Got your call waiting, it read. A quick check of the phone number told him it was a text from work. His stomach dropped. What if someone had found the missing staff page and he was in trouble?

> *Is everything okay?* Merridy texted back, hoping he was wrong.

> *Everything's fine. I'm glad I caught you. I was just handed a request slip for a band to spend the night in their practice room. It* must be Sarika texting him, then. As his supervisor, she should have been the only one contacting him outside of work anyway. Apparently, they're having trouble getting songs together for their first album and are running short on time. The higher-ups signed off on it, which means you'll be interacting with them on your rounds.

Merridy let out a relieved breath. It was only someone working late, which happened all the time. Sarika usually called to make sure he had advanced warning.

> *You know the drill. Check to make sure they're okay on every round through the building.*

This wasn't the first time a band had stayed overnight. Soul Sound had a nasty habit of passing out on their couches and not waking up until Merridy was gone the next day. Still, she was his immediate supervisor, and if he messed up she would be taking the fall. He understood why she had to double-check on him.

I'll make sure everything is fine, he texted in reply.

I'll leave you to the rest of your day, she finished with a small smile emoji.

Merridy closed his computer, putting it to sleep and forcing all other calls to go straight to voice mail. He pulled the blankets up to his chin and went back to sleep.

Chapter Three

Stan was already changing into his uniform when Merridy arrived at work. Given how much Stan hated his job, Merridy was always surprised how early Stan got to work. He hurried to catch up.

"Sarika contacted me too, kid," Stan called from his locker where he was picking out the crossword book of the day. "Let me know if they cause you any problems."

Merridy flashed a thumbs-up and nodded. Stan headed outside to the desk while Merridy finished buttoning and tucking in his shirt. He was right on time when he joined Stan in the lobby. Stan was busy situating his crossword book just right on the desk. He grunted again to acknowledge that he saw Merridy, so Merridy headed to the stairs. He stepped out onto the first floor and walked to Amaryllis's room, which was when he realized Sarika had never told him which band was staying the night. He would need to knock on every single door until he found the one with people behind it.

He had found no one by the time he reached the fourth floor, and a sneaking suspicion started creeping into his mind. Perhaps the reason Sarika hadn't given him the band's name was because she hadn't known it. The nameplate for the new band was still an empty space on the wall.

Merridy approached the final door on the fourth floor and had to pause outside for a very long moment to brace himself. There was no telling what he would encounter on the other side. He had to get it over with before he spent too much time on just one round.

The muted noise of people talking on the other side of the door stopped immediately when he knocked. Merridy waited, chewing on his lower lip, as the handle turned and the door was pulled open.

"Well, hello there," the man who'd opened it said politely. He had the faintest, almost musical Irish lilt to his voice. The smooth and even tone and the way his vowels rounded out of his mouth made it sound like he was singing every word instead of merely speaking. His hair was light blond streaked with purple that matched his eyes. He must have been wearing colored contacts, but the strange color worked really well for him. "Come on in, lad."

There were four other people in the room. Merridy recognized Director Rylee with a start that made his stomach drop to churn somewhere around his knees. He didn't know the other three men sitting on the couches, but they all looked anticipatory as Merridy stepped into the room. His stomach churned even more.

"There you are!" Director Rylee said happily. "We were starting to worry you had decided to skip this room."

Merridy swallowed nervously and thought about running back out into the hall. The band was obviously okay, so he should continue with his rounds before he got fired. The door clicked shut behind him before Merridy could bolt.

"We already know you wrote this, so don't try denying it," Director Rylee continued, his smile unabated. He held out a piece of staff paper so Merridy could see all the notes he had written, plus the band's additions. Merridy didn't say anything, holding his shaking hands at his sides. "But, you see, this is some of the most brilliant craftsmanship I've seen in over two decades."

Merridy's fists clenched involuntarily as his heart jumped in surprise. He was being praised? For abusing his position as a security guard and scribbling all over the band's music?

"Can you play this?" Director Rylee asked, holding out another piece of staff paper from the desk.

Merridy hesitantly stepped forward to take the paper, unsure about what he was being asked. It almost felt like an audition, except he still felt like he ought to be scolded instead.

The paper had a simple song. The music itself was minimal, one or two notes for each word, four beats per measure, and only the treble clef provided. There wasn't a time signature. The music read like a children's lullaby, but the lyrics promised something darker.

He could play it as it was. It would be almost too simple to pick out the scant notes on the piano with one hand. But that wouldn't do any justice to the music. He could already hear how magnificent the song could be with the proper chords. He walked over to the upright piano, placed the music sheet on the stand, sat on the bench, and gently rested both hands above the ivory keys.

Then he began to play.

He turned it into a faster song, almost an Irish jig inspired by the Irish tones he'd heard in the band member's voice. There were a lot of sixteenth notes for both hands and chords, but underneath all the flash, the original notes rang through the song. It needed a fiddle in accompaniment, but all Merridy had was the piano. He got through the first two stanzas, halfway through the song, when the strum of a guitar playing in harmony with his notes invaded. Merridy resolutely continued on, changing a note here or there to make the song work better as a duet. Together, he and whoever had joined him finished the song.

> *Faery dust and the rolling greens,*
> *A life of love, a love of thrills,*
> *We the people from under the hills*
> *Offer the sweetest of dreams.*
>
> *Ware, you be and you will live*
> *For the wee folk take all.*
> *Then laugh, happy as you fall,*
> *And our pains we never forgive.*
>
> *Of underhill and overstone,*
> *Lakes and rivers that always flow,*
> *Skies above and the caverns below,*
> *The faery court rules by blood and bone.*
>
> *Faery dust and the rolling greens,*
> *Devious, cruel, and oh so sweet,*
> *You should hope we never do meet*
> *Above, below, and always unseen.*
>
> *Tell me, how good is your luck tonight?*

It really was an eerie song. Mom had read him books about faeries when he was a child, but his interest in the supernatural had fallen by the wayside as he got older. Music was much more important.

He brought the song to a close with a flourish, then let his hands slowly drop from the piano and looked up. The band members' faces were impassive, although the one with red hair was staring at him. Only Director Rylee was grinning. Even the man just putting his guitar away on a nearby stand looked stoic. His hair was bright blue, as were his eyes. He was tall and imposing, yet the gentle way he had strummed the strings of his guitar told a different story.

"Tell me, Merridy, can you write down what you just played?" Director Rylee offered a blank piece of staff paper and a pencil. Merridy nodded, taking them. He found a space on the desk and started writing in notes on the paper. Some of the original notes from the first two stanzas had to be changed to accommodate the duet, but otherwise, he was able to write it note for note.

Director Rylee was beaming when Merridy put the pencil down ten minutes later. Without a word, he went and tugged on the open bathroom door, shutting it so everyone could see the poster taped to the back.

Merridy gaped at the picture of his father onstage, sweat gleaming in his red hair as he strummed a guitar.

"Your father is Lugh of the Tuatha Dé, isn't he, Merridy?" Director Rylee phrased it as a question, but it came out as a statement. Merridy couldn't do anything except nod.

That got a reaction from the band. The man who'd opened the door swore. "Damn it, Rylee. We've been looking for Lugh's son for how long, and you've had him right under your thumb?"

"I knew one of the two night guards had to be the one that left the notes for you, so I asked to use the restroom on my way out last night. I was able to search the break room and found your song inside. The man at the desk insisted he hadn't written the song and he didn't know who had left it there, which left only Merridy. I looked up his employee profile, saw his picture, and immediately figured out who he was."

"Are you really Lugh's son?" the blue-haired man asked. "We're the sons of Lir."

"I don't know how to explain it to you," Merridy signed, shrugging his shoulders.

"That's all right," one of the band members Merridy hadn't met yet said softly. He was the only one of the band without dyed hair. It was a much more natural reddish-blond color than Merridy's own bright-red hair. His eyes were very blue, Merridy couldn't help noticing, as his attention was focused solely on Merridy. "I can hear you just fine."

Merridy stared at him. That didn't make any sense at all.

"Lugh was a master of all trades," the man said, voice still soft. It was enchanting, as if every word he spoke was a spell of entrapment and Merridy his victim. "He could fight, he could lead, and he could play the harp like no other. A jealous woman spurned by the fact that his voice was prettier than hers cursed Lugh, stealing his voice for herself. What she didn't know is that many of the Tuatha Dé do not speak with words, but with thoughts. Lugh could not speak, but he could still communicate. He passed both traits on to you, Merridy Lughson."

Curses? Speaking with thoughts? It was all crazy. He didn't know who these people even were, let alone why they were spouting nonsense about him. Sure, Merridy was Lugh's son, the child of a famous guitarist, but the rest of the story was too strange.

"Ah, that's right. We never introduced ourselves," the man said. "I'm Fion, backup vocals and guitar. The guy with the purple hair is Aed, our lead singer; the guy with the blue hair is Fiachra, our lead guitarist—but we just call him Raven—and our drummer is Conn." Conn had hair colored red, purple, and blue. It was spiked into dangerous-looking points. "We're the children of Lir, High King of the Tuatha Dé Danann."

"They're Bard and Sons's newest band," Director Rylee added. "They're called Changeling's Court, and you, Merridy, are their final member."

No.

Merridy spun and pushed out into the hallway. He barely registered the door thumping shut behind him as he pulled in a whooping breath. Their newest...? He couldn't—he didn't—

He squeezed his eyes shut and breathed again. He had to go. He had to go do his job.

His job made sense.

He forced his legs to move, continuing on his patrol. He reached the door to the staircase and typed in the code, fingers sliding automatically from well-worn key to key, then headed upstairs into the cubicle farm.

An entire army could be hiding underneath the desks, but Merridy wouldn't have seen them. He went through all his usual motions, bending low to check for intruders while not consciously taking notice if he actually saw someone. He straightened from checking under a desk, and a drop of wet warmth splashed down on the back of his hand. Merridy stared at it as the drop slid off to stain the papers under his hand. He was crying.

And then, like a seal had been broken, he started sobbing. Tears dripped down his cheeks to stain the ugly carpet as he whimpered and sobbed.

They were offering him everything he had ever wanted: a band, a chance to play music, a chance to finally fulfill his calling. His last rejection still stung, mostly because they hadn't even bothered to let him play. When he hadn't been able to answer their opening questions with words, the band had kicked him out of their garage without even allowing him the chance to actually audition. This band, though... Changeling's Court. They were obviously crazy. It was all a cruel joke.

He wished they would have just fired him. It would have hurt less.

He reached the top floor of the building and paused in the open door of the stairs. Maybe he should just quit anyway. There were thousands of jobs that paid just as well. They weren't in any way affiliated with the music business, but perhaps it was time to let that dream go. The closest he had ever come to joining a band was tonight, and wasn't it sad that a joke was the nearest brush he'd had.

It wasn't meant to be. He had to accept that and find some way to move on.

"We didn't mean to crush your dreams," Fion said, sounding anguished as he rounded the corner of one of the executive offices and walked toward Merridy. "We just... Lugh said a mortal woman had borne his child and that the child would be more than capable of helping us defeat the Fomoiri. We were so excited to have found you. I'm sorry our introduction did not go better."

He was spouting more craziness. Merridy remembered Fomoiri from his mother's stories—the evil oppressors of Ireland, according to the mythology, but Fion was talking about them as if they were a current and pressing threat. Although, Merridy had also heard of the

Fomoiri in fairly recent musical terms, so maybe that was what Fion meant. Fomoiri were the band the Tuatha Dé Danann, his father's band, had constantly been getting into fights with. Were the Fomoiri getting back together and Changeling's Court had been formed to stop them? How petty.

Fion winced. "The Fomoiri are real enough, and their evil knows no bounds. It's not petty to want to stop them."

Merridy jumped in surprise and took an involuntary step back. His foot lost purchase on the stairs, and he stumbled, falling backward. Fion rushed forward and caught him, pulling Merridy securely against his chest and safely away from the stairs.

"I told you; you inherited Lugh's ability to communicate. I can hear you just fine without your finger speech."

That just wasn't possible. Reading minds wasn't real. People who insisted it was were probably con artists.

"I'm not a con artist," Fion insisted.

Merridy jumped again, this time kept from falling by Fion's strong arms. There was no way Fion could have gotten so specific a thought off Merridy's face. It was insane, he knew that, but... If—and that was a big if—he could read minds, that would make some of the other things he had said a touch more believable.

"We do want you in our band," Fion insisted, apparently reading where Merridy's thoughts were headed. "I'd be surprised if your performance before showed even half your talent. We could use someone like you to cut our record, and once you harness your full potential, you'll be a great fighter in the battle against the Fomoiri."

Battle? Like a battle of the bands?

"Look, we'll see if you're as good with the spear as Lugh. If you're not, then we can still use your musical talent. You weren't raised Underhill, so we can make allowances."

None of it was making any sense to Merridy. None of it at all. It felt like a really odd dream, and in a few minutes, he would wake up and realize he was late for work.

"Do you want to join our band? You'll be able to write music and play whatever instruments you want. That's everything you've ever wanted, right?"

It was, but the catch sounded pretty dangerous. Whatever battle Fion was talking about sounded like something Merridy didn't want to be part of. If Fion could read Merridy's thoughts, he knew that, but then he probably also knew the exact things to say to get Merridy to join. It was working. How could Merridy give up the chance to fulfill his dream?

"I'll join your band; that's it," Merridy signed, his fingers moving forcefully to show how serious he was. He would show his talent to the world, and when Changeling's Court became too weird, he would leave them and join a different band without all the extra baggage.

"All of that is fine," Fion answered, no doubt hearing the rest of Merridy's decision too. "Let's go tell Rylee."

Chapter Four

The band was still in their lounge when Fion brought Merridy back. Director Rylee was gone.

"Oh, good. You caught him," Raven said with a wide grin. Merridy knew what Lir looked like from all the videos and pictures he had seen of his father's band, and that grin was an exact match. "Rylee left this with us, but I can tell you haven't finished it. What else were you going to add before Rylee snatched it?" He was holding out a familiar piece of staff paper.

"I wanted to add one more note," Merridy signed hesitantly. His fingers were shaking slightly, but he reminded himself that he wanted this. They were crazy people involved in some sort of fight with another band, but they were also his opportunity to finally get his foot in the door and prove himself to the music business.

Raven studied Merridy's hands and frowned. "Your inner voice isn't loud enough for me to hear," he sighed. "Fion's the one with the ears. He'll need to teach you how to speak to us properly. For now, he'll be your interpreter."

Fion laughed, apparently unperturbed by being given a new job. "He'll pick it up quickly enough now that we've introduced him to the idea of it."

Merridy didn't like being spoken about as if he weren't there. He was used to it, of course. People always thought he was stupid just because he couldn't speak, as if one imperfection meant that there were dozens more hiding. Incensed, Merridy grabbed the staff paper out of Raven's hands and stomped over to the table to grab a pencil and finish writing the last note to the chorus.

"Ach, I didn't mean it like that, Merridy!" Fion gasped.

Then you should have damned well spoken to me rather than around me! Merridy snarled to himself.

"Ouch," Conn grumbled, rubbing his ear with one hand. The other was busy with a pencil, scribbling on a bit of lined paper.

"Yeah, loud and clear," Raven laughed.

"There are dozens of creatures in our world who can't vocalize words, but they communicate perfectly fine with their minds. I'll show you how, Merridy," Fion insisted.

Again with the crazy talk. Merridy hadn't signed any paperwork; he could leave right now and put all the crazy behind him before it was too late.

The door opened and Rylee walked back inside. He was holding the very stack of paperwork Merridy had just been thinking about.

"Don't sign it now," Rylee said as he handed the papers to Merridy. "Take it home, read it over, and actually take some time to think about everything these goofballs have told you."

Merridy looked at the paperwork and nodded slowly. He felt so unbelievably overwhelmed by everything at the moment that he couldn't think straight. The only thing that made sense was the music, and on the top of the stack of papers was a photocopy of the song he had just embellished on the piano a few minutes ago.

"Go home, Merridy," Rylee repeated.

"I have work," Merridy signed, clutching at the papers with his forearms to free his fingers. "I can't just go…"

Fion translated aloud and Rylee smiled gently. "Don't worry about that. I've already spoken with Stan and your supervisor. If you take the spot with the band, then they're prepared to look into hiring a new security guard. If you decide not to join the band, your position will still be available to you. So, take a few days and then come in sometime during regular business hours to let me know."

Merridy looked up from his papers. Director Rylee was still smiling slightly, as if Merridy's answer didn't really matter to him either way. Merridy wasn't certain that was true. Rylee was pretending it was, so Merridy felt he ought to as well. Fion was frowning, but he didn't say anything. He didn't need to; Merridy could tell Fion wouldn't willingly take no for an answer.

The rest of the band seemed interested, although not as much as Fion. Conn was still bent over his desk. Raven and Aed were both smiling, just like Rylee. There was an edge to their grins that Rylee had managed to keep hidden. They weren't happy about the possibility that Merridy might not join them.

Merridy clutched his papers tighter and nodded to Director Rylee. He turned and walked to the door, opened it, and walked back out into the hallway. He didn't stop until he reached the elevator, and then only briefly while he waited for it to open. This time Fion didn't follow him, and that was okay. Merridy had a lot to think about.

*

That night, Merridy tossed and turned in bed for hours. He wasn't used to sleeping during normal hours, which didn't help things, but he also couldn't shut his brain off. Every word, every nuance, was running through his mind. Had Director Rylee been telling the truth? Merridy could join the band? The paperwork Merridy had left on his kitchen table seemed to indicate exactly that.

Then there was Fion.

He'd seemed so sincere when he had chased after Merridy. He wanted Merridy in the band, but he was also involved in some sort of...fight? Merridy wanted to assume it was something as simple as a battle of the bands sort of drama, but something in the way Fion had snarled about the Fomoiri told a different story.

It wasn't long before he gave up trying to sleep. He sat up in bed and opened his computer, wondering if he could find some sort of answer online. The sudden light was shockingly bright in his three a.m. darkened bedroom. Once his eyes had adjusted, Merridy searched *Tuatha Dé*. A photo gallery of his father's band immediately popped up.

Lugh was easily recognizable. His red hair was vibrant against the rest of the band's blue, blonde, and green. The members of Changeling's Court had introduced themselves as the sons of Lir. He was the man standing next to Lugh with the blue hair, the exact same shade as Raven's. They looked like Lir, Merridy saw, with similar noses and eyebrows in addition to the distinctive hair color. The rest of Tuatha Dé didn't have any features in common with Fion, Aed, Raven, or Conn.

Merridy hit the Back button and scrolled through his search results. Most of the links were about the band, but there was one that had some stories of the mythical

Tuatha Dé, including one about some swans and the sons of Lir. Apparently in ancient times, a magical king of the Tuatha Dé Danann (the mythical people that worshiped the goddess Danu), who was named Lir, had three sons and a daughter who were forcibly changed into swans by a jealous stepmother. They lived in various lakes for nine hundred years, and only after a monk blessed them were they able to turn back into humans—after which they promptly died, because they were nine hundred years old. It read like a typical fairy tale and, given the band members had provided the same names as the characters in the story, was probably where Changeling's Court had chosen their stage names.

There was also plenty of information about the old fight between his father's band and the Fomoiri, mostly tabloids full of fistfights and angry words. Merridy didn't find anything about a battle until he went into the mythical side, where there were dozens of stories about the fight between the Tuatha Dé Danann and the Fomoiri. None of it really explained the battle Fion had been talking about.

There wasn't anything on the internet that would help him make his decision. Merridy sighed and pushed his computer to the side. He climbed out of bed and walked to his kitchen, where the paperwork was waiting for him.

It really came down to two issues. One, Merridy wanted to join a band and make beautiful music more than anything else in his life. Changeling's Court was talented, and Merridy knew that working with the band would catapult him into stardom. He didn't care that he was jumping into the group only thanks to his father's connection with their father—overusing connections was often how the music business worked—and he wanted to embrace the opportunity and see where the music would take him.

On the other hand, they were crazy. They were reading Merridy's thoughts and talking about going into battle. It wasn't normal, and Merridy wasn't certain he wanted to get involved with any of that. Music wasn't something to fight over. Drama muddied it for him, and this battle of the bands thing sounded too melodramatic and silly. Merridy didn't want to have anything to do with it, but if he joined the band, he would get embroiled. They would be living in close quarters, traveling together for months on end. There was no way to keep something as big as a fight separate from Merridy just because he didn't want to get entangled when they would be with him almost every hour of every day.

Merridy sank into a chair at his kitchen table, the stack of paperwork sitting in front of him, ruffled from all the times he had already read through it. On top was the photocopy of the song he had improvised on the piano. The notes of the duet he and Raven had arranged on the spot were staring at him. It was a beautiful piece. The notes rang through his head as he read through the song. Director Rylee had written *A Promise and a Warning* at the top. The title fit with the lyrics in the song, but Merridy couldn't help wondering what was being promised and who was being warned.

In the end, it really was a simple decision. They were offering him everything he had ever wanted in life. This was his chance to play music to his heart's content alongside people who appreciated it just as much as he did. There was no possible way to say no to an opportunity like that. Hopefully he could stay focused solely on the music and keep out of whatever craziness and fighting the rest of the band was involved with.

Merridy resolutely picked up the photocopied song and moved it to one side of the stack. Paperclipped on top of the contract was Director Rylee's business card. Merridy ran one finger down the phone number. It wasn't the number that went to the secretary's desk in the entrance hall. It wasn't even the number for the secretary who ran the CEO's floor where Rylee had his office. This was Rylee's personal number, and that wasn't something given out lightly.

They really wanted him.

It took a moment to find a black pen. Merridy knew where he was supposed to sign. Still, it was... This was big. Enormous. Merridy couldn't help looking at that black line for an extra moment before allowing pen to touch paper. His life was about to change forever. Merridy's heart was threatening to beat through his chest, and his throat was tight even as the pen swirled out the letters to his name. There were five different spots where he put pen to paper, promising his life to Changeling's Court and the Bard and Sons for the foreseeable future. As each one was done, he got a little more light-headed. It took him a few seconds to remember to breathe once every line had his signature, and he put the pen aside and restacked the papers neatly with a sense of lightness. It was relief. His decision was made and now... He put Rylee's business card back on top and let out a yawn. It felt as though a heavy weight had been lifted from his shoulders. He would go back to Rylee in the morning with his paperwork and finally start his life as a musician.

Merridy turned away from the table and back toward his waiting bed. Maybe now he would be able to get some sleep.

He was passing through his living room when he heard the clicking sound in the kitchen, as if his back door had just been opened. Merridy froze in place and listened hard. He didn't hear anything else, and yet there was a discordant note in the air that had him stepping back until he reached the fireplace. It was gas and Merridy never used it, but his mom had insisted that no fireplace was complete without a poker-and-brush set. He kept the heavy metal poker tucked out of the way in a corner, but it was easily the most dangerous thing within reach to grab. He held it in two hands with his back to the fireplace and waited.

The room was dark. Merridy had turned out the kitchen light on his way out and hadn't bothered turning on any other lights as he took the familiar path to his bedroom. Still, there was no mistaking the darker shadow that slid through the archway between the kitchen and living room. It almost oozed. It was oddly shaped, too, as if there were more than two arms and legs propelling it forward. It was searching for him, Merridy realized. He was standing still and it couldn't see him. It made a sort of sniffing noise, like a dog that had found an interesting smell.

Maybe it was all the strange talk about Fomoiri, but something inside Merridy was telling him that whatever was coming toward him wasn't human. He was also pretty convinced that it wasn't friendly, whatever it was, and Merridy wasn't going to like what would happen if it found him.

He gripped his poker in both hands and took a step toward the creature. It was either attack or run, and Merridy wasn't going to stand around waiting for it to find him. He crept closer slowly, feeling his way along the carpet so he didn't make any noise. He got near the creature and tightened his grip on the metal poker.

Suddenly, it spun and lunged. Merridy screamed silently and thrust his hands forward. He felt the pressure as the poker hit the creature and then the release as it slid through flesh. The creature gurgled for a long moment and then fell still.

Merridy dropped the poker and stumbled backward, nearly tripping over the coffee table on his way to the light switch. The overhead light flared on, making Merridy squint for a brief moment before his eyes adjusted. He looked over at whatever had attacked him and let out another silent scream.

Ooze was definitely the correct way to describe the creature. It looked like a greenish-gray slug with four arms and a defined, human-shaped head. It didn't have legs. The skin was black where the metal poker had punched through its chest, and that black was slowly spreading. It wasn't bleeding, and it didn't appear to be moving. The two eyes were closed.

Merridy gulped and swallowed air. None of the online pictures of Fomoiri had depicted a slug creature, yet what else could it be? There was only one way to know for sure. He was closer to the emergency phone in the kitchen than he was to his cell phone, so he scrambled around the creature and back into the kitchen. He pressed the On button for the phone's video screen, then paused. The police wouldn't know what the creature on Merridy's floor was, whereas Director Rylee actually might. If Merridy was right, and a Fomoiri had attacked him, then Director Rylee and Fion might be better prepared. Merridy grabbed the business card off the kitchen table and quickly tapped the number into the phone.

It rang twice before Director Rylee picked it up. A video didn't appear on the screen, which meant that function was unavailable on Rylee's phone. There was no way for Merridy to tell Rylee what had happened. He tried breathing hard into the receiver, knowing he probably sounded like a creepy stalker. He was already panting, so breathing forcefully into the phone wasn't difficult. Merridy also found that his hands were shaking. He gripped the counter to stop them, and his knees buckled. Merridy slid down to the floor, gasping for air.

"We're almost there, Merridy," Rylee's voice sounded from over Merridy's head where he had left the phone on the counter. "Fion heard you screaming. Two minutes. Stay safe."

Rylee didn't end the call, but he didn't say anything else. Merridy wrapped his arms around his knees and leaned back against the cabinets. He closed his eyes, saw the creature blackening in his living room behind his eyelids, and sat bolt upright again with a gasp. He was shaking all over now, unable to stop hyperventilating.

He had been attacked by some creature and he had killed it. He hadn't meant to kill it, but it had certainly meant to kill him. Why? All he had done was sign the paperwork to join the band. He wasn't part of their war and had no idea how to fight. Had the creature been waiting for him to sign his life away in order to kill him before he could join the battle? The obvious answer was yes, what with the creature's too-perfect timing.

"It's us," Fion's voice called as the front door opened. Merridy could hear the familiar creak of the hinges from the other room. He didn't use that door much at all, usually coming in and out through the garage door to his right. It was supposed to be locked, but then so was the back door, and the creature had come through that without any issues.

Fion appeared at Merridy's side a second later. Director Rylee was with him, but the rest of the band stayed in the living room, circling the creature.

Conn whistled. "I'd say he's got his father's touch with a spear." He sounded approving, but his words only made Merridy's body shake even more. "How'd you know to use cold iron to kill the blackguard?"

Merridy didn't have an answer. He definitely wasn't firing on all cylinders. His body was shaking and he was cold, and all he could see every time his eyes slid shut was that slimy body slowly turning a gray shade of dead.

"He's going into shock," Fion called. "Someone get me a blanket."

Who needed a blanket wasn't explained until Fion gently draped one over Merridy's shoulders. When had Merridy curled into a ball with his arms wrapped tightly around his knees? He couldn't remember.

"You've never even killed a fly in your life before, have you?" Fion asked softly. His arms were curled around Merridy over the blanket, and Merridy realized he was leaning against Fion's chest. It was completely different from being in Fion's arms when Fion had kept Merridy from falling down the stairs—Merridy was scared out of his mind this time, for one—yet at the same time, there was a sense of warmth and comfort that was seeping into his bones. "And here we are, asking you to jump headfirst into an ancient battle. I'm sorry we didn't understand how much we were asking from you."

Merridy's shivering slowly began to still under the combined onslaught of Fion's warm body and his gentle words.

"We'll do whatever we can to teach you to protect yourself from now on, Merry," Fion finished softly.

"Don't know that you can," Merridy tried to sign, although with his arms trapped by the blanket, he wasn't really able to make the correct movements. Fion heard him anyway. "I've never—" He paused and had to catch his breath before he could finish his thought. "I've never had to fight for anything before."

"You may be right," Fion replied with a heavy sigh. "We certainly weren't able to keep you safe tonight. We'll teach you the spear and see what magic you have, just in case. Okay?"

Merridy nodded. He was feeling strangely drowsy now that the initial shock was starting to wear off. The crazy thought of him learning magic didn't even faze him.

Someone started singing in the next room, and Merridy recognized one of his own compositions with a jolt. He struggled out of Fion's arms so he could sit upright and stare at the door separating him from the singer.

Merridy wrote music, but he didn't share it with anyone. He kept his most recent stuff in an unlabeled binder on the bookshelf next to the fireplace. Apparently, the rest of the band had been snooping through his things while he had been out of it. Still, despite his initial flare of surprise, Merridy couldn't help being calmed by the care and the skill whoever was singing imparted into each note. It was clear they respected Merridy's work and were honoring him with the song.

He started again when they launched into the second verse, singing with words this time—lyrics Merridy hadn't written, but which flowed into Merridy's notes and became one beautiful, melodic whole.

Chirping birds fly above as the sun rises bright in the sky

Singing out their mating call to the heavens far overhead

My window warms in the morning sun, but my heart is cold and my soul so alone

An empty bed, an empty house, an empty love, and an empty kiss

Where is my mating call?

Merridy was crying. Tears were running down his cheeks, and he was hiccupping with sobs. Fion's arms were circled around his torso again, and his nose was pressed into Fion's chest. The tears weren't because of the beauty of the song, not entirely.

The fact that someone actually liked his music enough to put their own hard work to his notes was so humbling. Merridy had never thought it possible that he would one day be able to share his music with someone, and he had certainly never thought it would sound as amazing as it did.

He was also crying because there was a dead creature decomposing in his living room and he was the one who had killed it. His life wasn't terrible, but it wasn't particularly wonderful either—he was mute, boyfriendless, and stuck in a job that paid him well, but he didn't particularly enjoy—and Merridy didn't know if the changes to his life that he had just agreed to by putting his signature on those papers were going to be even worse. So far, it was definitely worse, but with the song coming to a close in the living room, Merridy knew he couldn't say it wasn't better as well.

He struggled out of Fion's arms and to his feet. He wiped his face dry with a corner of the blanket wrapped around his waist as he walked to the doorway. He paused there with Fion hovering behind him.

The creature had lost what little sluglike form it had once had. It was now a lumpy blob of grayish-green that was rapidly turning black. The bits that had already turned black were flaking off like ash from a burnt log. Raven was holding Merridy's broom, and every time more of the monster came apart, he swept it into a dustpan being held by Conn. Merridy looked away from the sight quickly. Aed was standing on the other side of the room by the bookshelf with Merridy's thick music binder in his hands. He was slowly turning the pages, reading each song Merridy had written like it was one of the best books he had ever read. Rylee was standing next to Aed, ostensibly so he could read over Aed's shoulder, but he looked up at Merridy the second Merridy stepped through the door.

Rylee ran his finger across the binder in Aed's hands and smiled before turning to face Merridy. "The Bard and Sons would like to buy the rights for the song Aed just sang," he said. "One hundred thousand dollars for the song, and we'll also pay you royalties for future sales once the song has been released. I'll put it into a contract for you in the morning."

Rylee must really think the song would sell if he was willing to hand over an astronomical amount of money like that. Given the way Aed had just sung it, Merridy couldn't disagree. But handing it over for money seemed...cheap. He knew that was how the music business worked, of course, but why couldn't he hold partial rights to the song?

Fion dropped his hand on Merridy's shoulder before speaking. "You're buying it for the band, right?" he said, echoing Merridy's thoughts out loud. "So if he wrote it for the band he's a part of, why do you have to take it from him?"

Rylee's smile turned slightly smug, and Merridy realized this was a test. Had Merridy only been in it for the money and the fame, he would have jumped at the chance to sell his entire binder. Proving that he felt the music was more important had just won him some serious brownie points.

Fion had picked up exactly what Merridy was thinking, just like before. And Merridy had somehow known that Fion would hear what he was thinking about his music.

Maybe he could talk to them this way.

He turned toward Aed and thought hard at him. *What was the song you just sang?*

Aed jumped and looked up from Merridy's binder. "I heard you!" he said with an excited smile. "You are figuring it out. The poem was just a little something I wrote a few years ago, before I met my fiancé. It fit so well with your notes, I had to give it a try."

You made my notes sound beautiful.

"You made my lyrics sound beautiful, Merry," he answered simply, but his smile had grown.

"Merry can't stay here," Conn cut in suddenly. Merridy turned to look at him and saw that his dustpan was almost completely full. "They'll know their creature failed to kill him and will send more."

"Conn is right," Rylee added. Apparently, their discussion about Merridy's music was over. "Merridy, we have a secure compound a few miles from here. It would be best if you packed a bag and came with us."

Merridy looked at what was left of the monster and nodded shakily.

"We'll get you trained so next time they won't surprise you like this," Fion added.

"And we'll teach you how to really talk to all of us," Aed said. "Plus, while we're stuck together, we can work on writing more songs."

"Do you have any more binders of music you've written?" Rylee asked.

Merridy nodded. *In the spare bedroom*, he thought as hard at Rylee as he could.

"Lead the way," Rylee said with a smile.

All of his music stuff was stored in the spare bedroom. Merridy led them to the door and hit the light switch.

His two guitars, one electric and one acoustic, his upright piano, and an electric keyboard filled the space. He had a small desk with bookshelves on either side. The bookshelves were full of binders, each one as thick as the one Aed was still holding. They were all older notebooks; he put his newest stuff in the living room binder where he could go over it before work in the afternoons.

"We can pack up the guitars and the keyboard," Rylee said thoughtfully. "Those will fit in the back of our car with the notebooks. I'll have a van come for the piano in the morning. Is there anything else important to you that you don't want to leave behind?"

Aside from his computer, Merridy couldn't think of anything. He didn't understand why they needed to bring all of his instruments, though he appreciated the sentiment.

"Pack some clothes, enough for at least a week or two," Rylee continued. "We'll gather your notebooks."

Merridy suddenly wasn't certain whether Rylee was more interested in Merridy's notebooks or in Merridy.

Just because Merridy had proven that he wasn't in it for the money didn't mean Rylee himself wasn't. Still, Merridy knew that at some point in the future he would have ended up showing at least some of his work to the band. He decided that he would be flattered by Rylee's attention. He stepped out of the spare bedroom and walked down the hall to his own room. He winced at the state of his unmade bed and the piles of clean and dirty laundry on the floor. He quickly found a pair of clean jeans to pull on over his boxers and a shirt.

Fion walked into the room a moment later. "Rylee means well," Fion said. He sat at the foot of Merridy's bed as he spoke. "The problem with Rylee is he's spent far too much time Overhill, working in a human company with human problems. Sometimes he forgets himself. He's a good sentinel, though, and when he found the evidence that the Fomoiri were returning Overhill to amass another army, he contacted us immediately and was able to quickly set up the same cover story as our parents used in the last great battle to let us come here."

Merridy had a ton of questions to ask about everything Fion had said, but the biggest one was about how Fion had implied that Rylee and the rest of the group weren't human. Although, given the fact that the thing decomposing in Merridy's living room wasn't exactly something found in real life, maybe that shouldn't have been Merridy's biggest concern. Still, he couldn't help wondering what Fion was, since he certainly looked human. Merridy turned toward him to double-check.

Fion laughed. "Your thoughts are spinning so quickly. I know it's a lot to take in, but we'll all help you get through it. Let me see what I can explain right now."

He paused to think. Merridy turned away to dig through the closet for a duffel bag. He couldn't help wondering if there was a way to conceal his thoughts from Fion. Some things had to be private.

"First of all, we're not human," Fion started. "Many of us share the same basic form as humans—two arms, two legs, two eyes, etcetera—but we share little else aside from appearance. We call ourselves the Children of Danu, our goddess, but we are also known as Seelie Sidhe. Humans would call us faeries or fae. We have magic that allows us to be better and stronger than humans; we live much longer lives, and when we enter Overhill—the human world—we tend to stand out because of that. We have found the best way to remain hidden is to embrace the fact that we will be noticed by giving the humans a reason as to why they are so drawn. We are movie stars, famous singers, even athletes."

And the Fomoiri are the opposite? Merridy asked, although since he remembered exactly what the dead Fomoiri looked like, it sort of felt like a stupid question.

Fion looked frustrated for a second, but not as if he were upset with Merridy. "There's so much to explain," he said, "and I'm not entirely certain I can tell you everything properly."

It was quiet in the room for a few moments as Fion thought and Merridy packed away enough clothing for a few days away from home.

"There are many different types of Sidhe. Thousands, really, and most of them don't actually fit with anything I've just told you. Like I said, I am a type of Sidhe known as Seelie, but Underhill contains lesser creatures like dwarves, kelpies, sylphs, and much more who do not always resemble humans but whose powers still trend toward life and healing as Danu taught us." He paused and shook his head. A wry grimace crossed his face before he continued.

"There is a second side to Underhill, and this is the part you have to really understand. They are still known as Sidhe, but they are Unseelie, which means their powers trend toward death and destruction. The Unseelie also look human and have the same enhancements as the Seelie, but they are evil." This time his grimace was full of disgust. "Lesser creatures whose abilities and desires align with the Unseelie also flock within their court. The Fomoiri are one of those creatures.

"The part that is difficult to understand is when the Tuatha Dé first pushed the Fomoiri out of our part of Underhill, we were one. The distinction of Seelie versus Unseelie was unnecessary. Our great enemy was always the Fomoiri. When the schism in the Sidhe occurred, the Unseelie aligned themselves with the Fomoiri and now rule over them because they are lesser creatures. The Fomoiri would not have come Overhill without the Unseelie king's permission."

A Fomoiri could be anyone; they didn't necessarily look like a green, oozing slug. Calling them lesser creatures just because they didn't have a human form and were ruled, instead of being a ruler, was a little weird to Merridy, but he had a feeling that was because he was human and thought differently than Fion. What Merridy had to remember was that the two of them clearly were from different worlds, and he couldn't expect Fion to understand why that bothered him almost more than anything else he had learned so far.

Merridy also couldn't help wondering what the Fomoiri had done that made them the enemy. The one he had killed had certainly been after him, but Merridy had no idea why they were in a war and why that meant he had to fight.

"You are the son of Lugh, one of our greatest warriors," Fion cut in before Merridy could purposefully send a thought his way. "As difficult as it may be for you to believe, you are one of us. It is the sworn duty of every Seelie and child of Seelie to fight those who choose to follow the path of death. All those who ascribe to the Unseelie side of our schism revel in death and the pain of others. The Fomoiri you killed would have tortured you first, perhaps by devouring each of your limbs one by one. You would have begged for the release of death long before it was even offered in jest. Be grateful that you have some of Lugh's great powers and were able to avoid that fate."

Merridy didn't think a special power had allowed him to kill the creature, but he wasn't about to disagree with Fion when Fion looked as serious as he did.

"Almost ready?" Rylee asked from the doorway.

Just need to pack my laptop, Merridy answered. His duffel had been long packed while Fion had tried to explain everything.

"We've got your notebooks and instruments in our car. If you can put your clothes in your car and drive with Fion to show you the way?"

Merridy nodded. He felt like he was being steamrolled into all of this. His signature on the contract had obligated him to much more than was actually outlined there, and he didn't have a choice but to go along with it. He didn't doubt that more creatures like the one who had tried to attack him were on their way, so it was safer and smarter to go with Changeling's Court.

He just had to stay resolute. No matter what they taught him, be it the ability to speak with his mind or other sorts of magic, Merridy had to remember the music that had brought him into this fiasco. That was what was important here.

He lifted his duffel onto his shoulder and quickly packed up his computer and power cord into a separate bag. Once he was sure he had everything he might need, including wallet and keys from his bedside table, Merridy followed Rylee out of his bedroom. All evidence of the monster he had killed was gone, swept away somewhere. He didn't really want to know where, so he didn't ask. The contract was also gone from the kitchen table, he noticed as he walked through to the garage.

Fion turned out the lights behind Merridy and then followed him into the garage. Rylee trotted down the driveway to the SUV parked there. Conn was driving, and Rylee hopped into the passenger seat. Merridy put his bags into the back seat of his own car, got into the driver's seat, and started up the car as Fion settled into the passenger seat beside him.

Once Conn had cleared the driveway, Merridy backed the car out of the garage. He hit the button hooked to the sun shade to close the garage door, and then couldn't help looking at his little house for a few long moments.

For some reason, he felt as if he would never see his house again.

Would it be worth it if he got to play music? Absolutely.

With that thought firmly in mind, Merridy finished backing out of the driveway and then let Fion direct him through the quiet nighttime streets toward his unknown future.

Chapter Five

Merridy didn't want to open his eyes. He knew he wasn't lying in his own bed, and he remembered why, and all he wanted was to return to the oblivion of sleep for a little longer. His mind wasn't on the same page as his body, unfortunately, as he was still stubbornly awake.

With a sigh, Merridy finally gave in to the inevitable and opened his eyes. He rolled over in the queen-sized bed and looked out into the bedroom he had been given just a few hours earlier. Fion had walked Merridy through the massive mansion the band was using as their home base—not that Merridy had noticed much around him at the time. His head had been spinning, his body still shaky, and every time he'd closed his eyes, he'd seen the creature he had killed as it slowly decomposed into dust.

"Sleep, Merry," Fion had said kindly when they'd reached the door to Merridy's room. His eyes had been soft and full of understanding. For a moment Merridy had wanted nothing more than to beg Fion to stay with him, and Fion had nodded to say he would, but Merridy couldn't. As much as he didn't want to be alone, and despite remembering how warm Fion's arms had been at the top of that staircase, Merridy wasn't able to ask.

He barely knew Fion, which was certainly an important consideration. However, what really kept him from asking Fion to stay was the suddenness of the whole situation. One moment he was on his regular rounds walking in circles around an office building; the next he was killing monsters and in a band. He felt he was in a dream—or, at least, he had last night. As of this morning, Merridy didn't know what to think.

Everything was so different and he vaguely knew why, but at the same time he desperately needed to know more.

"Merry?" Fion knocked on the bedroom door, his voice sounding pleasantly curious, although Merridy thought he had probably heard every word Merridy had just been thinking. "Breakfast will be ready in about ten minutes."

Merridy took a deep breath and finally sat up. He rubbed his eyes to brush the last of the sleep away and reopened them to the scant light filtering in through the thick curtains over the windows.

I'll be ready, he called mentally, knowing Fion would hear him. Now he had to get out of bed. He resolutely threw back the covers and headed to the en suite for a quick shower.

Ten minutes later, he found Fion still waiting for him in the hallway. They walked through the vast mansion in silence. Merridy tried to keep his thoughts simple, but every time they reached another long hallway, or a flight of stairs, and they hadn't gotten to the kitchen yet, his curiosity jumped to the forefront of his mind.

Fion laughed softly. "Don't worry, Merry. We all know we have to answer some questions over breakfast. Let's just get some food in our stomachs first. All right?"

Merridy let a hand flow in front of him to sign his agreement, but he knew Fion had read his answer already. It was weirdly comforting in the same way that knowing Fion would have been willing to stay with him last night had been.

There would be no secrets Merridy could keep from him, but at the same time, there would be far fewer misunderstandings. Merridy could appreciate that in a relationship.

And there he went thinking those thoughts about Fion again. If he wasn't thinking about all of his questions, he was remembering Fion's warm arms. The fact that Fion had no doubt heard that last bit and didn't appear to object was another matter entirely.

Merridy snuck a look over at him, saw the happy smile Fion immediately sent his way, and knew that not only did Fion not care that Merridy was thinking rather salacious thoughts about him, but he kind of liked it.

They finally reached the kitchen, where the sweet smell of some sort of breakfast cereal bubbling on the stove filled the wide room. There were tall stools pulled up to the island, where Conn, Raven, and Aed were sitting.

Good morning, Merridy tried to say, concentrating on pushing his voice outward to everyone.

He received various iterations of "Good morning to you too" from the others in reply.

Rylee was ladling out bowls of what Merridy saw was actually oatmeal, although when Merridy sat on an empty stool and a bowl was placed in front of him, he could smell some sort of alcohol mixed in. It was good, anyway, and his bowl was half-gone far too quickly.

"So, you've got questions," Conn said as he dropped his spoon into his own now empty bowl.

He had so many questions, but now that the moment to get answers had come, Merridy didn't know which one to ask first. Did he want to know about the mansion, the band, the Fomoiri?

"Let's start at the beginning," Fion said, thankfully taking the onus away from Merridy having to actually form one specific thought into a full question. "Why did our fathers and the Fomoiri decide to create bands in the human world? I explained to you yesterday that humans are drawn to us, so we provide them with a viable reason for that. Humans are already drawn to their movie stars, their musicians; they wouldn't be worried about being drawn to us if we take on the same profession. It's also true that stars can move across the country—across the entire world—if necessary. If the Fomoiri were to suddenly go to Tulsa, we, too, could get on a plane and hold a concert nearby.

"We knew how much work being in a band would require, and that we had to do that work in order for the fiction to be believable—which would take time away from fighting—but it was an excellent cover story for our fathers then. When we came Overhill, it was easiest to recreate that. We unfortunately assumed the Fomoiri would do the same, but we are still waiting for confirmation of their whereabouts."

And the music? Merridy asked.

"Part of the cover story," Conn said. "You can't have a band without that band making music, and since we're all musicians of a sort, it helps pass the time while Rylee and our other Overhill informants work on figuring out the Fomoiri's plans. Lugh said he knew he had a child Overhill, but that the child's mother—while she didn't know about Underhill—had requested Lugh not take an active role in the child's life."

Merridy knew about that, although only from his mother's perspective. At the height of his career, Lugh had been a music star constantly on the move, and she had been only a groupie living the dream. There hadn't been a real relationship between them. Mom had told Lugh if he wasn't ready to make a permanent commitment to be there for Merridy every single day—which would have entailed his either taking them both with him wherever he went, or giving up his career—then she preferred he not be present at all.

Merridy wasn't certain he agreed with her decision, even now that he knew Lugh hiding the truth of Underhill from his mom was likely what had led to Lugh's agreeing with her dictate. Having any sort of father in his life, even one who showed up only periodically and left again all too soon, would have been nice, but it also would have caused a different sort of pain. Was the pain of not knowing his father worse than the pain of constantly being abandoned by him? Merridy couldn't say for certain.

Conn was still talking, so Merridy refocused on him. "Lugh knew he had a child able to navigate the world Overhill and would no doubt be proficient in music as all of Lugh's children are, which meant you could be of help to us. Lugh told us which city you were living in, so we set up operations here in order to find you, which happened far quicker than we originally expected."

Why do you have to fight them? What if you ignore the Fomoirians? What if all the Fomoirians wanted was to play music just like he did?

Conn shook his head for a few long seconds. "No. No way can we ignore them. For one, if we let them run rampant in the human world without confronting them, they'll get bored and start killing humans. I won't bore you with all the stories we have of that happening, but trust me on this. Plus, if we let them alone here, their masters Underhill will see it as Seelie weakness. They'll be emboldened to go after us Underhill. They kill enough big players Underhill, they could destabilize the monarchy and send Seelie into civil war. Thousands could die, and Unseelie could take over all of Underhill. Those powerful enough, they don't yet dare touch just yet—Lugh, for example—but they'll go after someone important to Lugh. Like you."

Me?

"They sent an assassin after Dian Cecht's grandson barely two months ago," Fion added. "Dian Cecht himself had to intervene. Now they've sent an army Overhill, and we're here to find out why."

An assassin? Merridy had to swallow hard on that one. Was that what the green blob creature in his house had been? Merridy looked over at Fion, but he only grimaced at Merridy instead of answering.

What do we do? Merridy asked.

"We wait," Rylee cut in. "This house was purchased by the previous band and is for the use of our fighters should they need to come Overhill. While the spies and informants start digging in, we must begin preparing ourselves for what comes next. This includes readying music if we need to use the band as cover, so that is your task today."

Merridy definitely liked the sound of that. He scraped the last mouthful of oatmeal out of his bowl and swallowed, then eagerly looked at the rest of the band.

"Can't argue with a face like that," Aed grumbled good-naturedly as he grinned at Merridy's hopeful expression. "Come on then."

*

Over the next few days, Merridy quickly learned Conn liked to think in drumbeats. The band sat in comfortable couches around a long coffee table in one of the sitting rooms with sheet music, scrap paper, printed lyrics, and abandoned pencils scattered all around them—and Conn tapping constantly on the table to the beat of whatever song they were working on in the moment.

> *A solitary song, trilled high above to the scuttling clouds,*
>
> *The second bird on a wing replying in earnest as they meet amid the gusting winds.*
>
> *Here on the ground, me with my feet firmly planted in the earth,*
>
> *A lonely heart, a lonely blanket, a lonely life, my lonely being.*
>
> *When will my mating call come?*

Aed didn't say much. At times, he seemed almost irritated with the entire process, shifting unhappily on the couch as if he was constantly impatient with sitting still and waiting, and yet when he sang the simple notes Merridy had penned in conjunction with his lyrics, even Conn's fingers fell silent. It was impossible not to listen, and Merridy's heart soared with every beautiful note. Merridy was that solitary bird, calling out for someone to hear him and desperately hoping for an answer.

Fion's shoulder brushed his almost unintentionally as he leaned forward toward the piece of staff paper where they were writing in Fion's harmony, yet the timing with

Merridy's last thought said otherwise. Merridy looked up at Fion just in time to catch him hastily looking away. His cheeks were faintly pink, and as Merridy watched, Fion briefly looked away from the staff paper to glance at Merridy out of the corner of his eye.

Merridy couldn't help leaning closer until their shoulders were purposefully touching, but he only picked up a pencil to tap the spot where a D note could be written in. Fion didn't pull away, and the warmth of his body settled comfortably against Merridy.

"Should we sing a D there, or should I play that chord?" Raven asked. He didn't have his guitar in his lap at the moment, since there wasn't space for it at the table, but it was leaning behind him, against the back of the couch, where it would be in easy reach should they need it.

"Why can't we do both?" Fion countered. "This ballad needs to be simple and easy to contrast with the other songs on the record. There's no need to add too many notes."

Conn snorted unhappily, and his fingers drummed down on the table, *one-two-three-four* before he sat back in his chair and crossed his arms. "The song's too simple. I'll barely need to hit a snare for a beat."

"Maybe for this song, sure, but we're going to have plenty of other songs with a ton of drums." Raven had his own arms crossed, and he frowned heavily at Conn.

"Right." In that one word, Conn sank all of his disbelief and disdain, and Raven growled at him and snapped something back in reply.

Merridy closed his eyes and breathed it all in, reveling in the music he could hear growing between the five of them. Every note they put down, every squabble they overcame, all came together in a wonderful crescendo that made his fingertips tingle and brought an involuntary smile to his face. This was what he had always wanted—every failed audition, every wish hidden in his heart, he had yearned for something exactly like this.

Fion's body shifted next to Merridy, and suddenly a warm arm was draped over Merridy's shoulders and Merridy couldn't help leaning into that heat. His head fit comfortably against Fion's shoulder, and it was good. Far better than any other man Merridy had ever tried cuddling with before—but then, no other man had ever smiled at him the way Fion did either.

"And I'm glad for that," Fion said softly, his lips brushing gently over Merridy's hair.

A knock sounded on the studio door before Merridy could still the thumping of his heart in his throat and answer. Rylee opened it a moment later and stepped inside.

"Lunch will be ready in five," he told them, but his eyes were already straying down to the table to look at what they had been working on.

Aed didn't need to be told twice. He hopped to his feet and left the room before the rest of them had even sat all the way up. Conn was next on his feet, and he clapped Rylee on the shoulder as he followed Aed.

"Nothing's ready yet," he told Rylee on his way past. "Give it another week and we'll have something for you."

"I'll be waiting. You think Merridy will be ready to move on to proper fighting then too?" Rylee called after Conn, who paused in the doorway to look over his shoulder at Merridy, whose stomach started churning.

Conn grinned at him, and it was so lighthearted that Merridy let out a breath of relief. "We'll see. Merry's coming along nicely, but music will always come before fighting for him. Right, Merry?" He didn't wait for an answer, instead continuing on toward lunch.

Merridy didn't want to leave the comfort of Fion's arm, nor did he want to leave the comfort of the sitting room with the music scattered on the table and saturating the air around them, but he knew the day would keep moving along regardless. Besides, as the rumbling in his stomach attested, he was hungry.

Fion walked with him to the door, where Merridy paused to look back at the table where Rylee was carefully looking over their notes. They wouldn't return to work on their songs today, which was a shame, because they had really been getting somewhere with "Mating Call." The afternoon was instead spent in the weight room, where— as Conn helpfully put it—Merridy was "getting rid of his scrawny."

The music would still be waiting for them tomorrow, and that surety allowed Merridy to leave it behind for the moment, although it would take more than physically leaving a room for the notes to ever leave his thoughts.

Chapter Six

The piano keys were hard and cold under his fingers until his touch brought warmth to the ivory. The pedals vibrated under his toes as he pressed, and the sounds of notes held and blended with chords filled the room. Merridy wasn't playing anything specific, instead letting his fingers stroke along the keys as they willed. It was calming, and Merridy very much needed calm at the moment.

Still, after a few more bars, his fingers began to slow and the music to ebb. When his fingers finally came to a stop, Merridy wasn't exactly calm, but his nerves had eased.

"I won't ask if you remember what you just played, because I know you've memorized every note. We add a guitar line to that, and some drums..." Fion trailed off from where he had just appeared in the doorway, his eyes closed in bliss as he no doubt imagined what that would sound like. Merridy could hear it, too, and he liked it.

It still needs words, he thought at Fion.

Fion shrugged. "We'll figure it out eventually. We're getting close to being ready to go back to the studio to start cutting an album."

That news had Merridy's heart jumping back into his throat. It was amazing. First, they'd cut an album and the single they were going to release to the radio, then wait as sales started and they planned a nationwide tour. He could almost envision being on the road as clearly as the music.

It was a real shame music wasn't their only purpose here.

As if he had read Merridy's thoughts—which he probably had—Fion let out a sigh and nodded.

"We're ready for you now," he said softly.

Merridy stroked his fingers across the tops of the piano keys. He didn't press down, but the cool comfort the keys gave him was enough to get him on his feet. He walked to where Fion was waiting in the doorway and followed Fion out of the room and down the hall.

The music half of the mansion the band was occupying was on the far side of the building, part of a series of private rooms and studio space. While the rooms were technically supposed to be soundproof, noise did leak out, which could disturb any other occupants of the mansion. At least, that was the reason Merridy assumed the music rooms were tucked away. The workout rooms were similarly placed, except the gym was on the exact opposite side of the mansion.

Merridy had been spending far too many hours at that damned gym lately. Walking miles around a building at night might have kept him skinny, but Merridy had quickly learned there was a big difference between being skinny and being in shape. The running, jumping, and lifting weights had definitely humbled him, and yet in a way, the exercise was almost as exhilarating as the music he had just been playing. The movement, the rhythm of working out flowed through him the same way the strings of a piano did. Merridy had been surprised to learn he didn't hate it.

But he already knew he was going to hate what they were going to make him do today.

"You don't know that, Merry," Fion cut in sharply. "Just because the only time you've speared something gave you a few nightmares doesn't mean you'll automatically hate using the spear."

Stay out of my head, Fion! Merridy snapped, despite knowing the futility of asking that and, if he were being honest with himself, despite not really wanting that at all.

"Stop thinking so loudly, then," Fion replied firmly, but the small grin Merridy saw on his lips said he had heard the second half of Merridy's thoughts too. Merridy tried not to blush and focused on keeping his thoughts on those piano keys and the peace that had come with playing. It didn't quite work, but fighting to keep his thoughts in line helped pass the time for the rest of the long walk to the other side of the mansion.

Conn was the only person in the very large room set up as a gym. One wall was entirely comprised of mirrors, and the other three were thickly padded. The floor also felt spongy under Merridy's feet from even more padding. Off to the right were the free weights and weight-lifting machines Merridy had been using exclusively for the last two weeks. Off to the left were racks of weapons Merridy had been avoiding.

"Here you go," Conn called as Merridy walked toward him. He was holding out a long wooden pole with a metal cap on one end. It wasn't an actual spear, since the metal was flat instead of pointed, but the heft and width of the pole would emulate it. Merridy swallowed hard before reaching out to take the mock spear from Conn.

He was surprised to find the weight felt right in his hands in the same way the weight of a guitar did. Merridy hadn't expected that. He stared at his fingers where they were closed comfortably around the wooden shaft and tried not to feel like they were betraying him.

"You didn't have to be taught how to play the piano," Fion said, his voice almost hesitant, as if he was afraid to answer the questions Merridy had been thinking. He must know his words were hastening the shattering of Merridy's residual calm. "You put your hands on the keys and created music. It's Lugh's gift, and you share it. Merry, you share this gift too."

How can violence be a gift? Merridy thought toward both Fion and Conn. His eyes hadn't moved from his fingers, and since he didn't really want to see their expressions at his question, he kept his gaze where it was.

"There's at least two sides to any war," Conn replied. "There's the people who attack first and the people who defend themselves from that attack. In our war, the Fomoiri are the aggressors. You are the protector; you are one of the people who will keep that aggression away from innocents. To be able to protect like that is the greatest of gifts."

"It's also one of the greatest burdens," Fion added. "One we understand weighs heavily on you. But, Merry, to understand the burden you're forced to bear means you also have the compassion to realize that to save the innocents you have to kill, you have to hurt a creature who, until the moment you allied with us, had held no ill will toward you. It shows the strength in your heart, and we prize that more than your ability with the spear or with a piano."

Merridy shook his head in denial, but his thoughts returned to one worry that had been bothering him ever since the Fomoiri had appeared in his living room.

I've never met a Fomoiri before. How do I really know they're the aggressors, that they're as evil as you say they are? And how do I know the people you say I'm protecting are really innocent?

"That's..." Conn trailed off and ran a hand through his multicolored hair as he frowned at the floor. "Saying that's how it's always been doesn't give you a real answer, but it's true. From the first moment the Sidhe and the Fomoiri met, we have fought, and it is because of the cruelty and evil of the Fomoiri that the Seelie Sidhe have continued to keep watch and to take up arms when the need arises."

"The fact is, Merry," Fion added, "you've already chosen a side. It's too late to return to neutrality." He sounded genuinely sorry, and his eyes were earnest when Merridy looked up at him. "Let us teach you how to protect yourself, at least. If you decide you can't agree with us and leave, you'll be safe."

He reached out, as if he wanted to rest his hand comfortingly on Merridy's shoulder. Merridy carefully kept his thoughts inside his own head, because as much as he wanted the warmth and comfort Fion's hand would give him, part of him still wanted to hold on to the stubborn fear that what Fion was doing was wrong. Merridy wasn't a fighter. He played music because the notes called to his soul. It wasn't right that the spear in his hands called to him too. There was no reason holding a training spear should feel as natural to him as touching the keys of a piano.

There was too much going through Merridy's mind, swirling and spinning, and it was all so confusing. The anger from earlier had faded away to nothing, but so had the piano-induced calm.

"A spear is more than just a throwing tool." Conn's voice cut through Merridy's thoughts. Merridy blinked and refocused on the wood between his fingers and on Conn watching him carefully hold the practice spear. "You used a thrusting motion to defeat the Fomoiri in your house. A spear can also be defensive when used for blocking like a regular staff might be used. Thanks to your heritage, you already know all this instinctively. I'm hoping to connect your instinct to your will, so you can be as prepared with a spear as you are when suddenly handed a new piece of sheet music."

Merridy hid a grimace along with his thoughts and hefted the training spear. *What do I need to know?* There wasn't much point in protesting or refusing to learn. Fion was right that Merridy had to learn how to protect himself. It might be possible that everything he was being told about the Fomoiri was a lie. But he had played music with the entire band, and he honestly couldn't believe that the people who put so much soul and heart into the music they made with him would turn around and lie to his face.

"You have your hands in the right places. I'm going to attack, and all you need to do is bring your spear up to block. I'll fix your footwork and technique as we go."

Merridy took a deep breath and nodded, steeling himself for what was to come, and then brought his spear upward when Conn began.

*

"We can't stay hiding in this mansion forever," Aed grumbled. He threw the sheet music the band had been going over down onto the coffee table in front of him.

Merridy reached to pick up the pages, happy to read through the next verses of the song that had originally drawn him into the band. They were hoping to release it as their first single.

> *Dinner at five; party's at six.*
> *Across the room, I see your smile.*
> *You're not looking at me.*
> *You haven't, not for a while.*
>
> *Broken heart, the tears I've cried,*
> *I'm done with all your lies.*
> *Oh, yes, I'm done with your damn lies.*
>
> *If a butterfly don't fly, it falls.*
> *You are my wings; you are my wings,*
> *Broken wings, shattered, torn.*
> *You are my wings, and I'm breaking free.*

"The Fomoiri aren't going to wait for us to show up before they attack. They're out and about, no doubt doing something terrible, and we're sitting here writing songs." Aed scowled at the table where Raven had abandoned his guitar pick and Conn had dropped a pair of drumsticks. Merridy put the sheet music back, but kept his thoughts to himself.

Rylee let out a heavy sigh and shook his head. "Aside from the suspicious activity that made me call you in, I haven't seen anything. They're obviously here, or they wouldn't have attacked Merry, but I have no idea what else is going on."

"We need to find out," Aed replied immediately. "Go out there and start digging, see if one of them slimes out of whatever sewer they're hiding in."

"It's never a bad idea to be proactive instead of reactive," Conn agreed.

Raven shook his head. "We don't even know where to start looking. We'd just be running around out there like chickens with our heads cut off."

"Oh, come on! We have to do something!" Aed jumped to his feet and swung his arms around the room as if the comfortable couches they were sitting on were evidence they weren't doing enough.

There was a cadence to their argument, a beat of sorts. *Dum, dum, dum.* It was slower than a heartbeat, and intense. Not the big bass drum or the lighter tom-toms. More like hitting the side of the drum for the effect. Merridy couldn't help pulling a clean piece of staff paper over to jot down the beat.

Drums were difficult to write, mostly because there were so many different types of drum to use. They were also completely dependent on the meter—which all music was, admittedly—but when in a band, the drums often set the meter for the song, which meant Merridy's notes had to be even more exact.

He kept writing as the argument continued with Rylee reminding them all that he hadn't been able to find any further sign of the enemy, which only made Aed snarl more.

The beat began to change tone in Merridy's head. Instead of from an argument, it began to take on a clacking sound: the noise of wood impacting wood.

High block, middle block, low block. Repeat! High block, middle block, low block.

And then there was the double clack of Merridy retaliating in turn, and the amount of beats he was penciling onto his paper doubled per measure.

High block, high strike, middle block, middle strike, low block, low strike. Repeat!

It was amazing and rather frightening how quickly Merridy had been picking up the art of staff fighting. The weight with a spear was different than with a staff, of course, and thrusting and throwing a spear were just as important, but those lessons weren't what he wanted to put onto paper at the moment. Except he couldn't help adding another line of sixteenth notes for an electric guitar rapidly descending down the scale like the shot of adrenaline that hit when he lined up for a throw.

Fion glanced over at Merridy, and his lips quirked upward into a smile before he opened his mouth and sang:

The battle, the fight, so eager for blood,

The kill, the triumph, the will to stand tall,

Of bodies and screams, you hear none of their cries.

Of pain, and of death, look at the soaked ground you stand on.

Oblivious,

Your heart calls for conflict, never realizing those you hurt as you strive.

Oblivious,

Your soul dreams of the next mountain, not remembering those you left behind.

Oblivious.

Fion's voice didn't quite have the sheer power of Aed's, which was why Fion was backup vocals, but his tone was clear and pure, and his words managed to hit the beats exactly as Merridy had been writing them. It was a clean song, stripped down at the beginning with only the drum and the words, until that guitar riff came in with the chorus. The first "oblivious" ran down the scale like blood dripping from a dire wound. The second rose upward again, soaring in falsetto like a choir of angels welcoming home the recently dead. The third was almost a whisper, as if the cold winds of sorrow swept across what was left in an empty field filled with the bodies of the fallen.

It was exactly the way Merridy felt after the adrenaline from wielding a spear faded away and reality returned—his exact emotions and fears put to beautiful, haunting music.

Fion had managed to take Merridy's simple drumbeat, combine it with the images it had evoked inside Merridy's head, and release it to the world for everyone to hear. Merridy couldn't help the flutter in his heart or the hitch in his breathing, nor could he stop the fervent wish to kiss Fion from growing. Fion didn't look at Merridy, but he must have known where Merridy's thoughts had gone—he had read every other serious thought booming inside Merridy's head from the first moment they had met. Without an outward reaction from Fion, Merridy fought to suppress his want. It was one thing to share warmth or smiles, or to laugh together like friends, but if Fion didn't want him as more than that, then Merridy wasn't about to embarrass himself over it.

The rest of the band and Rylee were all gaping at the two of them. Aed shut his mouth first and shook his head. "Fine. We don't have to attack right now. But we need to keep digging to figure out what they're up to."

"Agreed," Rylee added, recovering from his own shock quickly as he leaned forward to look at the staff paper Merridy had been writing on. "How about a compromise. Leave the mansion and come to the studio. We can get a few songs recorded, since you're supposed to be a real band. And that will let whoever is watching know we're here and we have no interest in hiding away from them. Entice them to make the first move."

"It's too late now," Conn cut in when Aed tensed like he was about to jump to his feet and head to the door. "First thing tomorrow morning. Eight o'clock in the van. Bring your weapons and your instruments. It's definitely time to have a little fun."

Chapter Seven

"I think we need to talk," Fion said softly the next morning. They were the only two sitting at the breakfast table. Conn and Rylee had both come to eat and gone, and neither Aed nor Raven had appeared yet. It was only seven, so they still had plenty of time to get ready.

We do, Merridy agreed. The awkward silence after their impromptu song the previous night flashed through Merridy's mind. As if he needed the reminder. He had only spent the entire night tossing and turning in bed, reliving the way Fion had completely ignored his feelings. It was better to talk it out right now instead of letting it drag on. The sooner Fion turned him down properly, the sooner Merridy could begin the process of getting over his crush.

"Ach, Merry, please," Fion said with a groan. "Being Overhill for this long is crazy enough for me. I never expected to even find you, let alone like you. All the stories our dads used to tell me of their time Overhill, and then I'm assigned to take their place up here." Fion leaned closer to Merridy as if he were about to divulge a secret and didn't want anyone to overhear. "Lugh approached me before I left and told me to keep an eye out for you. He was never able to come back Overhill after his assignment ended—it's really difficult for the more powerful of us—but he always wanted to. He wanted me to find you and, if you were willing, to bring you Underhill to meet him. But, Merry, then I actually met you."

Merridy had absolutely no idea where Fion was going with his rather rambling monologue, but there was almost a sense of desperation to it. It was as if even Fion didn't really know where his thoughts were headed.

"I hear you, Merry. I've always heard you, even when you aren't actually speaking to me. You sing in my head, the most beautiful sound I've ever heard. I heard you as you were approaching the door to our practice room for the first time, and knew I wanted to learn more about you. But you're Lugh's son. I was tasked with finding you and bringing you to meet your father. Having feelings for you wasn't an option. But the more time we spend together and the more you sing in my head, the more my conviction fades." He huffed a sigh and looked up at Merridy. "Merry, I don't know what I'm supposed to do anymore."

How could Merridy answer something like that? It sounded like Fion did like him, but was holding back out of some sort of fear of Merridy's father. Merridy didn't know Lugh. Pictures on the internet and stories from his mother didn't give life to the man in Merridy's mind. Fion, on the other hand, did know Lugh well. It was entirely possible his fear was founded.

"No, no, it's really not. It's all in my head." Fion sighed heavily, staring down at the table as if the glossed wood grain had the answers. "I'm afraid of what Lugh might say or do to me if he knew about my feelings. He was basically a second father when I was growing up. My own father had duties as high king that kept him away, and Lugh was always there to take up the slack."

High king? Merridy couldn't help gasping in surprise. Fion might have mentioned that before, but Merridy had had other things on his mind then. Did that mean Fion and the rest of the band were princes?

Fion laughed, and suddenly the heavy air in the kitchen caused by their conversation vanished. "Underhill doesn't work that way. Honestly, I don't think anyone really knows how Underhill works at all. You see, Nuada was king for a long time, but then he lost his arm, and Underhill somehow decided he wasn't king anymore because of that. Lir became king sometime after. When Nuada's arm was healed, he became king again. Lir obeyed the whims of Underhill and let it happen. So, no, I'm not a prince at all."

Underhill sounded like a very interesting and very strange place. Merridy wouldn't mind visiting sometime. He would like to meet his father too, of course, but seeing all the wonders Fion was talking about sounded amazing. First, though, all he wanted was to make music. Merridy was not exactly excited to participate in the whole convince-the-Fomoiri-to-attack-so-Aed-and-Rylee-could-figure-out-where-they-were-hiding-and-what-their-evil-plan-was.

Fion reached across the table to take Merridy's hand in his, gripping tightly enough that Merridy felt grounded in reality again. Merridy gripped back, and although he hadn't quite learned how to hear thoughts the way he could send them, he heard as much as saw Fion's happy smile.

"Ready?" Conn called from the doorway.

If I have to be, Merridy replied slowly. He glanced down at his hand still held in Fion's, then up to Fion's very blue eyes. He gathered strength from their connection and from the way Fion was still smiling at him before reluctantly pulling away to follow Conn to the front door.

"Here," Conn said when they reached the door. He held out what looked like a foot-long metal cylinder. "You press down this button here," he explained while demonstrating, "and flick your wrist like this." He flicked his wrist hard to the right, and suddenly the cylinder elongated like an umbrella shaft until it was about five feet long with a sharp, pointed end. "It's not as long as a proper spear, and it's not as strong." Conn tapped the center of the spear where the metal overlapped. "A good hit here will bend the metal, and you won't be able to close it again. Still, it's cold iron, so any hit by this will hurt a Fomoiri, and if you grip it on the end and throw it like a proper spear, it'll cause some real damage." He flicked his wrist the other way, and the spear collapsed back into the small cylinder. Then he held it out to Merridy.

It took Merridy a long second to work up the courage to take the spear from Conn, but when he did, he immediately had the warped, awful feeling of the weapon fitting perfectly into his hand. He knew its heft despite the fact he had never practiced with such a short spear, and he could easily envision how to grip it for defense and how to hold it for a proper throw. It was the same feeling he got every time he placed his fingers on the keys of a piano or the strings of a guitar, and he hated the comparison between something that brought life—brought music—to the world and something that brought death.

"Life and death are two sides of the same coin," Fion said softly as he joined them at the door. "To give life, sometimes you also need to know how to take it. If you never know pain or loss, how can you write a song to help someone heal after experiencing that in their own life?

Merry, how could you have written something as powerful as 'Oblivious' without first holding a spear and feeling the emotions that go along with it?"

As usual, Fion had read Merridy's thoughts and soothed his fears. Merridy didn't return the spear to Conn—although he was still tempted. Instead, he turned toward Fion and held out his free hand so they could walk hand in hand out to the waiting van.

"Keep your eyes open for trouble," Aed said as Rylee drove down the mansion's long driveway and turned onto the main road.

Merridy sat on the edge of his seat, one hand gripping the seat belt where it lay across his chest, and tried to keep his breathing even as nerves fluttered like butterflies in his stomach. He hadn't been out of the mansion since the attack at his house, and he had no idea what to expect. There was a weight on everyone's shoulders, and the entire ride was completely silent. Aed, Conn, Raven, and even Fion were visibly tense, their eyes darting along the road, missing none of the cars and pedestrians they passed along the way.

It was almost a letdown when they reached the Bard and Sons without running into anything worse than slow traffic at the stoplights. Walking into the familiar building almost felt like returning home. Merridy had spent so much of his life here, had spent so many hours walking through the halls wishing for a chance—just a moment to prove himself musically—and here he was, walking through the front doors with his band. It was surreal.

He waved to Brice and Jimmy on his way to the elevator. He knew both guards fairly well, as they were the ones who replaced him and Stan when their shift was over. They waved back, looking genuinely excited for him.

The elevator dropped Changeling's Court off on their floor, and it was a quick walk from there to one of the recording studios.

Merridy had been inside the studio hundreds of times, yet for some reason, he was nervous. Raven and Fion both set their guitars on the stands provided for them. Conn immediately went to the drums, trailing his fingers gently over the metal rim of the tom-tom. There was an upright piano Merridy would use resting against one of the walls, but he couldn't make his feet move from the doorway.

Raven and Aed had turned their backs to him despite the fact it left them looking at the wall. Merridy appreciated their kindness because he was shaking and that fear was embarrassing. This was his dream, and now that he was about to see it realized, his feet were rooted to the floor.

Conn grinned at him from the other side of the room. "It's damned scary the first time, isn't it? I'm shaking." He held out one trembling hand to prove it. "We've worked damned hard these last few weeks to get our music ready, and I am so worried we'll mess it all up."

After putting his guitar down, Fion returned to Merridy's side. He wordlessly held out one hand—offering his support and to share his strength. Merridy wasn't too proud to turn that down, and with Fion's warm hand in his, he finally stepped all the way into the room.

The hard keys of the piano were cold to the touch, but they provided even more of a calming effect. Merridy finally took in a deep breath—he hadn't realized he had been panting in fear until the moment his lungs finally opened and he could pull in a full breath of air—and let it out again slowly.

Okay, we can do this, Merridy said firmly, projecting his words to the entire band.

"Good to know," Rylee's voice called through the overhead speaker system. He was standing on the other side of the glass, in the control room. "You guys finish getting set up, and I'll get everything ready out here. We can run through the song with everyone playing and singing, and when I listen back, I'll decide which parts need to be run through solo. Let me know when you're good to go."

The first song they were planning to record was "If A Butterfly Don't Fly." It definitely fell into the alternative genre, with heavy guitars and Aed's raspy singing voice, but it was still soft enough to be a ballad and potentially be released as a pop song too. "Mating Call" was pure pop, but "Oblivious," when they had a chance to finesse that song, would be exclusively rock. They would have an interesting mix of songs on their finished album, but today was all about getting "Butterfly" ready to drop as their first single.

Merridy sat at the piano bench and then hit a few keys experimentally. The notes chimed and their smooth sound filled the room. Once everyone was plugged in and everything was tested, they played.

> *In my dreams, I know you see me,*
> *And in my hopes, you'll hold my hand.*
> *Reality hits, so does the truth:*
> *You and me will never be we.*
>
> *Another dream, a hand on my shoulder,*
> *Someone smiling only at me.*

You're laughing, so happy.
Reality hits, and I'm still alone.

If a butterfly don't fly, it falls.
You are my wings; you are my wings,
Broken wings, shattered, torn.
You are my wings, and I'm falling hard.

Dinner at five; party's at six.
Across the room, I see your smile.
You're not looking at me.
You haven't, not for a while

Broken heart, the tears I've cried,
I'm done with all your lies.
Oh, yes, I'm done with your damn lies.

If a butterfly don't fly, it falls.
You are my wings; you are my wings,
Broken wings, shattered, torn.
You are my wings, and I'm breaking free.

After they had all settled down at the mansion and started working on music, this was the section of the song they had worked on first. They'd already had the basic melody fleshed out with the soaring harmony and the discordant notes for emphasis, but this verse was different. The words evoked the same feelings Merridy had had when walking out of the Bard and Sons with a stack of paperwork in hand and a promise in his ears: scared to leave behind the past he knew, yet excited about the prospect in front of him.

His fingers stroked along the piano's keys, pressing slightly softer in memory of that hope.

> *Flying without wings, I should fail.*
> *The ground should near; pain should invade.*
> *A hand on my shoulder: it's not a dream.*
> *Who's watching me as I once watched you?*
>
> *Hope in my heart, you're with me.*
> *Can I hold your hand? Please don't leave.*
> *Reality hits; you're still here.*
> *You and me will always be we.*
>
> *If a butterfly don't fly, it falls.*
> *You are my wings; you are my wings,*
> *Broken wings, shattered, torn.*
> *My wings can soar, and I'm flying high.*

Merridy found himself involuntarily looking over at Fion as the last notes of the harmony faded away in the room. He was already looking at Merridy over his microphone, and his eyes were bright with emotion. He knew what the words meant to Merridy thanks to their conversation at breakfast, that having Fion in his life allowed Merridy to feel like he was capable of leaving his worries and fears behind and flying free.

"That was amazing, guys. Let's get another take just like that, and then we'll strip it down to voices and piano." Rylee's voice interrupted the quiet reverence in the studio. Merridy blinked and looked away from Fion, but the connection between them didn't fade.

Chapter Eight

The sun was already setting by the time they walked out of the Bard and Sons again. They had left their instruments in the now-locked studio, since the plan was to come back tomorrow and the day after and the day after that until the Fomoiri finally showed their hand. As they all piled back into the van, though, Merridy could feel how much lighter the atmosphere between them all was now, in comparison to the drive in. The music had done what music was designed to do—soothed their worries and calmed their fears. Even Aed was laughing at a joke Raven had just told.

It didn't take too long to drive back out to the far suburbs where the mansion was located. The streets were darker, the streetlamps more spread out and hidden amongst trees just beginning to lose their orange and yellow autumn foliage, and there wasn't a lot of traffic.

One moment, they were driving along, jovial from a wonderful day and looking forward to finding dinner, and the next, something massive rammed into the side of the van.

The seat belt cut into Merridy's chest as it punched him back into the seat, and his arm slammed into the door next to him. Somehow the van didn't flip, but the engine died with a pained splutter. Something roared outside, and metal screeched as long claws dug into the door next to Fion and ripped it free.

"Fomoiri!" Rylee snarled, then swore when the seat belt holding him in place didn't pop free.

Fion's head hung low, and blood dripped from a cut on his scalp. He must've been knocked out, which meant he was completely defenseless to whatever was on the other end of those claws.

The spear was in Merridy's hand before he even realized he needed it. With a quick flick of his wrist, it elongated to its full five feet. Something growled outside— Merridy could see the reflection of light in six pairs of closely placed eyes as the creature peered into the van.

He gripped the spear at the end and threw.

The thing howled in pain, and the eyes vanished. Aed, Raven, and Conn jumped over Fion, diving out of the van after it. Rylee slashed open his seat belt with a knife and was out his door half a second later. Merridy unhooked his own seat belt, then reached for Fion, but his fingers froze before he could actually touch Fion's shoulder. If Fion had a back or neck injury, the last thing Merridy should do was jostle him.

Fion? Fion! Merridy called in the loudest voice he could, directing his thoughts to Fion specifically so he didn't distract the others. A pained screech sounded outside, and Conn roared in triumph, so the battle was apparently going well. *Fion!* Merridy called again, and this time Fion groaned and slowly lifted his head. He blinked blearily for a moment before a rumbling growl from outside made him jump. He swore and grabbed for his seat belt.

"Come on, Merry. We have to go help," he said as his fingers scrabbled for the release button.

But your head! Merridy gasped.

"Is fine enough to fight. They need us at their backs and able to defend ourselves, not as sitting ducks they have to protect." He finally got the seat belt unhooked and climbed out of the van. Merridy couldn't help following, more scared to be alone in the van than out on the edge of the forest in the middle of a battle.

The thing he had thrown his spear at was lying next to the car. It was massive, easily the size of the car, and extremely hairy. Merridy had to step on it to get out, and as he passed by, he gripped the jutting end of his spear and yanked it free. The dead flesh of the creature underneath the cold iron was already blackening, especially around the sword wound in its neck that must have been inflicted by one of the others.

Other bodies dotted the landscape around the car, and none of them looked remotely human. Many had multiple arms and legs, or had no discernable body shape, like the slug creature Merridy had killed in his house. The rest of the band members were all engaged in their own battles with even more of the creatures.

Fion let out a fierce yell and jumped into the fray. A gleaming sword suddenly materialized in Fion's hand, and he wielded it as proficiently as he did a guitar, slicing into enemies with abandon.

The hard beat of their newest song rang through Merridy's ears like a battle chant. The words had never been more poignant than they were now, as blood of many different colors spilled on the pavement of the road and the leafy debris of the forest. Fion hadn't looked back at Merridy since he'd jumped into the fight.

Oblivious,

Your heart calls for conflict, never realizing those you hurt as you strive.

Oblivious,

Your soul dreams of the next mountain, not remembering those you left behind.

Oblivious.

There was a growl behind Merridy, and he spun around, the spear automatically at the ready. A creature with four arms and one cyclops-style eye was barreling down on him. All four arms had two-inch-long, serrated claws, all of them pointed in Merridy's direction.

Using the spear was instinctive. He didn't need to think about it as he gripped it toward the back and thrust upward, point first. The spear was longer than the creature's arms, and the second the tip touched its chest, the creature let out a howl. There was the slightest resistance as the spear slid home, slicing through the creature's chest as if there weren't any bone or other matter to stop it. There might not have been, but Merridy was having a hard enough time keeping his lunch down.

"Merry! Watch your back!" Conn yelled. Merridy spun around, but he already knew he was a beat too slow. The new creature was more snakelike, and it had slithered up behind Merridy silently. Twin fangs were bared and already descending as Merridy futilely fought to free his spear and bring it around in defense.

Fion appeared, stepping in between the snake and Merridy. His sword struck, and the creature crumpled to the ground, the too-close fangs scraping down Fion's shoulder as it shuddered in its death throes.

Even in the scant light from the car, Merridy could see Fion's face go white as pain immediately set in.

Fion's hit! Merridy called to the others. *I think it's bad.*

Conn was at their side a second later, a giant mace in his hands and a worried frown on his face when he caught sight of the dead Fomoiri and Fion's wound. It was just the barest scrape, no worse than a skinned knee on the playground, but the skin around the scrape was already turning the dark purple of a bruise.

"The house is that way, just through the trees," Conn said, pointing in the direction they had just been driving. "Fion knows where the antivenom is kept. You two go. We'll hold the line here, keep them distracted to give you time to escape. Go!"

Fion struggled to his feet and resolutely turned toward the trees. Merridy rushed to his side, ready to catch him if he stumbled, and they both hurried into the dark forest.

It was hard going in the dark with leaves slippery from evening dew and roots and sticks jutting up to trip them. Fion kept walking forward, doggedly heading toward help. Merridy trailed slightly behind him, spear at the ready.

"It's not bad," Fion said softly, no doubt in response to the worry Merridy was having a lot of trouble keeping bottled inside. "It's not an outright bite, so the venom is only from the residue on the Fomoiri's teeth. I'll be fine."

Let's hurry. The sooner they got back to the mansion, the sooner Fion could take the antivenom.

They walked on for a few more minutes with just Fion's increasingly harsh breathing puncturing the silence around them.

Then the quiet was broken by a growl to their right. A second growl joined it, and something cackled gleefully to their left. This time, Merridy heard the slither of scales on leaves from behind them.

"We're surrounded," Fion said flatly, glancing around them even as he brought his sword to the ready. "We'll have to fight our way free..." he trailed off, his eyes fixed on something on the forest floor just to his right. "Or we can escape Underhill. Come here, Merry!"

Merridy obeyed, and when he got close enough to Fion, he could see a circle of white mushrooms poking out from between the dried leaves on the ground.

"Step inside. Don't squish a mushroom," Fion instructed, then followed word with deed by striding forward and placing his feet carefully in the center of the circle. Another growl sounded, this one closer. Merridy jumped into the circle with Fion and felt a strange sort of tug near his belly button. The forest vanished from around them—the last thing Merridy heard was a defeated cry like a hawk's screech—and was replaced by an empty field of tall grass and a warm summer sun blazing overhead.

Was this Underhill? Merridy looked around them, and though he knew his mouth was hanging open, he couldn't spare the attention to close it. This place was so amazingly beautiful. The way the wind whispered through the grass and the birds chirped so sweetly was completely unlike anything he had ever heard before. He wanted to close his eyes and revel in sheer delight, but Fion's pained groan reminded him of why they were here.

Now what? They were in an entirely separate world from the mansion—and the antivenom. How were they going to find something to help Fion all the way out here? The field of grass looked like it went on for miles in every direction, and there was no sign of anyone.

"Now we walk. Keep thinking about finding someone to help. Underhill will hear you even more clearly than I do, and will see us to wherever we need to go." Fion reached out and gripped Merridy's hand in his. "Don't let go. If we get separated here, we may never find each other again." The tightness of his grip also told Merridy that Fion needed the emotional support to help fight off pain.

Merridy squeezed back, and together, they started walking.

Chapter Nine

Merridy had no idea how long they had been walking. The field went on forever, the view unchanged no matter how many steps they took, and the sun overhead hadn't moved. Merridy tried to keep the thought of finding help at the forefront of his mind, but it was hard when worry for Fion and the rest of the band kept intruding.

Was everyone okay? There had been even more creatures hidden in the woods, waiting for them. What if Conn and the rest tried to follow Merridy and Fion and fell into the same ambush? Hopefully they would follow the road to get back to the mansion.

Where they would immediately find that Merridy and Fion hadn't made it back. No doubt they would rush into the woods to start a search.

The only way to save everyone else was to get back to the mansion as quickly as possible, and they couldn't do that until Fion was well enough to show Merridy the way out. He needed to get Fion help, fast.

He looked up from his feet and almost stopped walking in surprise. Only Fion's continued tugging on his hand kept him moving forward. They were back in a forest of some sort, although Merridy hadn't seen any trees on the horizon, and he certainly hadn't noticed the transition between grass and leaves under his feet. He looked over to Fion to ask what had happened but kept his thoughts to himself when he saw Fion's jaw clenched and the tight wrinkles on his forehead from pain.

Merridy could ask all of his questions when Fion was well again.

"That looks a bit nasty," a voice said suddenly from Merridy's other side. Merridy jumped, and Fion stopped walking so they could both turn to look at the stranger, who was a tall man with bright-blue eyes, leaning against a nearby tree. "This is one of Lir's get, if I'm not mistaken. And with hair that red, you must be one of Lugh's. I'm one of Dian Cecht's great-great-great-and-so-forth-grandchildren. Don't ask me how many greats are there, because I honestly don't know."

Why are you here? Merridy asked sharply.

"The real question is, why are you here? Since Underhill brought you to me, I can assume you need some healing, which I can see Lir's child does desperately need."

He was bitten by a snake Fomoiri.

"Their venom is quite potent," the man said in agreement. "Come along. I've got a bed we can put Lir's child in. You can call me Quinn, by the way."

Fion might have been in incredible amounts of pain, but he didn't seem worried about Quinn. Rather, it was Fion who turned to follow first, and Merridy had to hurry behind before their clasped hands pulled Fion off-balance.

"He's a healer," Fion gasped between clenched teeth.

Merridy didn't really know what healer meant in terms of being Underhill. Was it like a doctor with antivenom and stitches, or was there magic involved? He could only hope for the best as they walked along the forest floor. A rough path appeared after about a minute, and they followed it for only five minutes before a large building came into view. It was three stories tall, with wide windows along the front. Every single window was brightly lit, and the front door was open to the warm afternoon breeze.

"Welcome to my inn," Quinn said with a pleased grin. "I've got an empty room you can use for the night. By morning, you should both be ready to head back to wherever you came from." He led the way up to the front door.

"Don't eat anything," Fion said sharply, his hand squeezing Merridy's tightly before letting go for the first time since they had arrived Underhill. "It's not safe if you don't know where it came from. Don't leave the inn without me, or Underhill might grab you away."

"If it does grab you, fix the image of my inn in your mind and start walking," Quinn cut in. "Underhill will bring you back here. Now, up one flight of stairs, if you would. Room's the door to the right."

Fion obeyed. Merridy's stomach tightened with worry when he realized Fion's bad arm was held stiff and unmoving to his side.

"I'll get him fixed up," Quinn said softly, with a gentle smile for Merridy. Merridy didn't know if Quinn had read the worry from his face or his mind. "I prefer to run my inn and hide out here in the middle of nowhere, but that doesn't mean my lineage doesn't ring true. Lir's boy I can fix up, and with a few hours' rest he'll be on his feet easy enough. You, on the other hand, I don't have a cure for. What that witch took from Lugh was passed on to you; until Lugh solves his own curse, I'm afraid you're without a voice."

I can speak well enough, Merridy replied.

Quinn's lips lifted even more into a grin. "That you can. Come on in and find a seat. I'll get you when Lir's son is healed." He hurried into the inn after Fion, and Merridy followed.

The first floor of the inn was a typical common room straight out of a medieval movie. There was a long bar on one side with a thick wooden top, and scattered throughout the room were round tables with rough chairs surrounding them. The fireplace off to the side had a wide mantel, and the floor was thinly covered with rushes.

Merridy took a seat at an empty table and waited, hoping Fion would be okay. He wanted to go upstairs and check, but at the same time, he didn't want to interrupt Quinn and maybe make things worse. There really wasn't a good way to tell time, what with the sun still being overhead in the same exact position as when they had first landed in the grass, but he guessed it was at least two hours before someone came downstairs. It wasn't Fion or Quinn, but a stranger, followed by two other people, a woman and a man, all of whom glanced at Merridy without interest.

A few minutes later, four people walked in the front door and took seats at separate tables around the room. Two people, a man and a woman, pushed through a door at the back of the room. The man stepped behind the bar and started filling drinks while the woman moved to the seated tables. She was a waiter, the same as any restaurant might boast, except her skin was flower-petal pink, and her ears were so big and pointed they towered a few inches over the top of her head.

Merridy was hungry, but he trusted Fion's warning, so when she turned to head toward his table, he waved her away.

Another hour passed excruciatingly slowly. Merridy had to remind himself over and over again not to go upstairs and was tapping his fingers impatiently on the table just to keep his anxiety somewhat contained.

"You a bard?" someone asked. It took Merridy a second to realize he was the target of the question. "You're tapping your fingers in exact time to the sounds of this inn." It was one of the men who had come down from upstairs. He had the same style ears as the waiter, but his skin was purple. Together they looked like something out of an Easter egg poster.

I can play some instruments, Merridy replied, eager for anything to distract him.

"I have a Crwth. You ever played one of those?" He reached under his table and pulled out a slim, square box. He unhooked the clasps and pulled out a wooden rectangle about two feet long with strings across the middle like a guitar. There was also a bow.

I haven't. You have a piano?

The man grinned. "This is Underhill. We always have a piano." Two other men jumped to their feet and went around to the far side of the bar. They rolled out an upright piano and settled it next to Merridy's table. Merridy moved his chair over to sit in front of the piano and gently stroked his fingers across the hard keys. He could only think of one song that probably originated from Underhill—the song Rylee had had him play as an audition on his last night of work as a security guard—so he pressed down on the first notes of the song.

The rest of the inn's patrons recognized the song even with Merridy's embellishments, and within seconds the entire room was singing along.

Faery dust and the rolling greens,

Devious, cruel, and oh so sweet.

You should hope we never do meet

Above, below, and always unseen.

Tell me, how good is your luck tonight?

The stranger was quick to pick up Merridy's melody and harmonize on his Crwth, which was played sort of like a violin with the base pressed against the front of the shoulder instead of under the chin. The song came to a close on that last, ringing question, and the final chord rang through the inn.

"Beautiful! Beautiful!" Quinn said as he descended the stairs into the room. He was smiling, clapping with the rest of the inn.

How is he? Merridy asked, immediately jumping to his feet and rushing over to him.

"Come up and see," Quinn replied easily. He waved toward the stairs, and Merridy hurried up. He turned right at the top and found the first door. It was propped open, and Merridy could see Fion lying on the bed inside. Merridy walked in quietly, in case Fion was sleeping, and leaned over him to look.

The bruised shade of purple on his shoulder was gone, as was the scrape from the snake's tooth. It took Merridy a few seconds to realize that Fion's chest wasn't rising and falling. He wasn't breathing at all.

Fion! Merridy grabbed his shoulders and shook him. Should he try CPR? Had the venom been too strong? Merridy shook him again.

"That won't help," Quinn said from behind him, his voice soft and somehow menacing. Merridy spun around, his hand going to the collapsed spear tucked into his belt. "Neither will that." Quinn looked pointedly at his hand.

What did you do?

Quinn shook his head, as if he were a sad parent disappointed in Merridy. "Here I thought I had a son of Lir and a son of Lugh fall right into my lap. Underhill finally answered my call and sent me two people to join my cause and spring me from my forced exile. After all, who wouldn't be more interested in revenge on Nuada than Lir and his children, who were tricked out of the crown, and Lugh and his child, who were tricked out of the second-highest position of power in all of Underhill? Or so I thought. When I asked this son of Lir for his support, he denied me. So now I'm asking you, son of Lugh: Will you support my cause?"

Merridy couldn't help noticing that Quinn had yet to use either of their names. Maybe he didn't know them, but it could also be an Underhill thing. Merridy didn't see any reason to tell Quinn their names, given he was apparently crazy.

What did you do to him? Merridy asked.

"He's not dead. At least, not yet. I put him into a form of hibernation. He's breathing, but so slowly your human eyes can't see it. If you want him to continue breathing, you're going to take your little spear there and go deliver an important message for me."

What's the message? Merridy couldn't keep the reluctance out of his voice, but Quinn didn't appear to notice, given his cheery grin immediately reappeared.

"See, I knew you would be happy to support my cause. Your first mission is simple: go have a chat with

Dian Cecht. He's been distracted lately by some new grandbrat of his suddenly appearing. I expect your chat might end a bit violently, preferably with the tip of your spear in Dian Cecht's heart. Understand? Lir's son and I will wait here for news. Double-cross me and it will only be me waiting."

How will I find Dian Cecht?

Quinn walked around Merridy to a small nightstand near the bed. He picked up a small photo lying there and handed it to Merridy. It was of a mansion easily double the size of the massive one he had been sharing with the band, with colonnades all around and what looked like a bell tower off to the left.

"Keep that image in mind as you're walking, and Underhill will know to take you there. As to how you'll recognize Dian Cecht, look for the man with the most intense blue eyes there. All of Dian Cecht's line have them, but the magic will be strongest in his."

Merridy looked into Quinn's own very blue eyes and only saw that they were cold and hard. Then Quinn's bright smile filled his face again, and his eyes lightened with happiness. It really was an amazing act—one Fion and Merridy had both fallen for.

"You should go now," Quinn said with a genial wave toward the door. "The sooner you go, the sooner you can return here and see whether Lir's son survived the night."

Merridy hurried out of the room, down the stairs, and out the inn's front door. He couldn't stop or look back because he was worried that if he did he would march back up to Quinn and punch him in the face. There was no way that would end well for Fion.

There was only one option: go find Dian Cecht.

Merridy wanted to save Fion more than anything, but he had absolutely zero interest in killing someone. And if

Dian Cecht was really as powerful as Merridy felt safe assuming he was, then killing him, or even attempting to kill him, would no doubt end very badly for Merridy.

There had to be another way. There had to be something else he could do.

Except all he knew how to do was play the piano and stab someone with his spear. Since the latter was out, he had to find some way to play. The man back at the inn had said there was always a piano around in Underhill, so all Merridy had to do was convince someone to allow him to play in front of Dian Cecht and Merridy would play a song that told Dian Cecht what was happening. All Quinn's spies—if he had any—could report back was that Merridy had played the piano; there would be zero sign of him double-crossing Quinn that way.

The plan hinged on Dian Cecht actually listening to Merridy's song and understanding what Merridy was saying, which wasn't a given, but it was the best plan he had.

Merridy fixed the image of Dian Cecht's home into the forefront of his mind and started walking, desperately hoping that whatever he found on the other end wouldn't lead to his and Fion's deaths.

Chapter Ten

Dian Cecht's home was massive. It wasn't a big mansion like Merridy had thought—it was a castle. The colonnades he had thought he had seen in the picture were actually decoratively ribbed outer walls of the castle with soldiers patrolling on top. The camera angle for that picture must have been extremely skewed. It was the only explanation for such a drastic difference.

Merridy steeled himself and walked up to the front gate, where a guard holding a heavy lance stopped him.

"What's your business here?" she asked politely, albeit firmly.

I'm a bard. I was hoping to play here tonight? Merridy answered. It was the only thing he could think of that might get him through the door.

"Fourth one tonight," the woman's partner, a man with a sheathed sword at his hip and a sour expression on his rather pointed face, said, before spitting off to the side.

"Then the master's table will have plenty of entertainment tonight," the woman responded easily. "Go on in, boy. Follow the path to the right, and you'll arrive at the kitchens. Someone will come find you there when it's your turn to play."

Merridy hurried past the guards and easily found the path in question. The main road was paved with stones and led up toward a huge front doorway. The smaller path leading to the kitchen was also paved, but it was rougher. Merridy followed it and found himself walking through a kitchen garden. There were pole beans and trellised cucumbers to his right, and to his left were different kinds of tomatoes. Farther on were beds full of herbs and some other vegetables. Merridy had never been big on gardening—he was much more interested in spending his free time with his instruments than playing outside—but he had to admit it smelled really nice. None of it helped his rumbling stomach, of course, but Fion's last words kept him from snagging a trailing bean.

Quinn had already hoodwinked him once. The last thing he wanted was to get hurt by ignoring Fion's warning, and then not be able to save him.

The kitchen itself was at the end of the path. Merridy walked inside and into utter chaos. People were running around frantically, screaming instructions at each other, and it was general bedlam. Merridy had to stay in the doorway to avoid getting trampled. Somehow, despite the craziness, he could see platters of food heading toward the doorway on the other side of the room.

"You another bard?" someone asked from Merridy's right. A larger woman was standing there, her arms crossed and a streak of flour across her cheek and her very orange, flat beak of a nose. Merridy nodded. "You'll stay out of the way until you're called. Either stay outside or stay in that corner." She pointed behind her, to a very small area where three people were already sitting.

I'll stay outside. Merridy backed out the doorway into the sweet-smelling garden, and the woman vanished back into the chaos.

He was so damned tired of waiting. His stomach had stopped rumbling at this point, no doubt because it had started eating itself. He was also thirsty from all the walking in the sun, although now that he was thinking about it, he noticed the endless day had apparently turned to dusk.

And the best part was that Merridy had absolutely zero idea of what he was going to do when he was called to play. He'd tried to think of lyrics as he was walking over, but that had distracted him from keeping the image of Dian Cecht's house in the forefront of his mind. Besides, lyrics had never been his strong suit. That was more Aed, Fion, and Raven's specialty.

Someone in an official-looking uniform walked past the kitchen door inside, and a few seconds later, crossed back in front of the door with one of the bards following him into the rest of the castle. Over the next few hours, as the sun very slowly set, the next two bards were also called away. Merridy knew he was next, but he still didn't know what to do, and then the official was standing in the kitchen door looking out into the garden for him.

Merridy followed him inside.

The chaos in the kitchen had slowed, and the sweet smell of chocolate filled the entire room. It was now thankfully easy to slip through the kitchen and through the far door. The hallway beyond the kitchen was narrow with gray stone walls. They walked past a number of side halls, turned right, and then went up a short flight of stairs that led into the back of a long hall filled with three equally long tables.

Each table was stuffed on both sides with people chattering and eating. The diversity in the colors of their skins and their general features was amazing to see.

Women with massive horns, men who took up three seats because their shoulder and hip bones were that wide, and other individuals who were so unique Merridy couldn't tell if they had a gender at all. There were feathers and bones and even fangs everywhere he looked. It was beautiful, in a strange sort of way.

On the far side of the room was a raised dais where four people were sitting. Merridy wasn't close enough to see if one of them was Dian Cecht. Next to the dais stairs was an upright piano with a scratched lyre sitting on top.

Merridy sat on its bench and pressed his fingers against the piano keys, and with that calming touch, he suddenly he knew what he had to do. He just had to play. He couldn't put words into his songs—he couldn't even sing them—but music was emotion put to notes. He could put his fear and worry, everything weighing down his mind, into the piano.

Maybe, hopefully, his message would get across.

Merridy pressed down, and music rang out. He closed his eyes and concentrated on each individual note and chord. Fion's gasp of pain when the Fomoiri had nicked him. The purple bruising. His expression of pain. The relief of finding someone to help amid the strange world a mushroom circle had brought him to. And then, the betrayal and the horror of seeing Fion lying there. He poured everything into the piano, and it sang under his fingers as each hammer hit the strings.

When Merridy finally brought the song to a close, he somehow felt lighter. It was as if his worries had floated away as every note faded into the air. His head was spinning slightly, too—or maybe that was the room spinning around him.

The room was also completely and utterly silent. Merridy slowly looked up and realized that every single eye in the room was staring at him, people's desserts and conversations apparently forgotten.

"Now that is a true bard, I would say. Bard, I invite you to play for me privately." The new voice came from the dais. "A little after-dinner entertainment in the salon sounds wonderful. Bard, please rise and join me."

Merridy could see a man standing on the dais, but he was still too far away to make out exact facial features. It could be Dian Cecht standing there, but he had no way to be certain. Still, he stood to obey.

The room suddenly slid sideways in his vision, or maybe that was his body tipping sideways. It was really hard to tell the difference. Then everything went black.

*

"A nasty combination of far too much stress for a prolonged amount of time and a lack of proper meals for almost twenty-four hours." The voice was silent for a brief moment. Merridy had no idea who was speaking or where he was, just that he was waking up. He was lying on something soft, so apparently someone had moved him from where he must have fainted.

"I know you can hear me, so you might as well open your eyes."

Merridy started and opened them slowly to find the green canopy of a four-poster bed over his head. Someone was sitting to his left, so he turned his head to look and met a pair of blue eyes so vibrant they seemed to glow in their owner's face.

Dian Cecht.

"Yes, I am Dian Cecht. Your story at the piano, bard, was beautifully done. You will no doubt be glad to know that I have already sent a force to speak with my rather errant grandson. Your injured lover should be safely brought here within the next hour, where I can easily heal the damage. So, then the question becomes, what sort of bard are you?"

Dian Cecht paused, looking at Merridy as if waiting for an answer. It took Merridy a moment to formulate his thoughts into actual words. He still didn't know where he was or what had happened, and now Dian Cecht was saying exactly what Merridy wanted to hear: that Fion would be safe. Still, after trusting Quinn, could he take a chance at trusting another stranger?

Dian Cecht seemed to understand Merridy's hesitation. He smiled gently at Merridy and leaned back in his chair as if he wanted to give Merridy as much space as possible.

"You see, those of us in Underhill all have a love of music. A tone-deaf Sidhe is almost unheard of, even in those whose line is cursed as yours is. That said, the number of us that are capable of putting magic of such power into play simply by interacting with an instrument is sadly very small. The entire dining hall saw your story just as easily as we heard it. Lugh has only had two children that he knows of, and only one has human heritage. Isn't that correct, Lugh?" he asked, turning his head to look over his shoulder.

Merridy had been so engrossed by Dian Cecht's sheer presence he hadn't even noticed that someone else was standing by the doorway. Merridy turned to look and saw a near-mirror image of himself. The bright-red hair color was exactly the same as Merridy's, as was the general shape of the face. There were differences, of course, but there was no doubt that Merridy was looking at his father.

Hello. Lugh signed in ASL with his fingers and spoke with his mind. *I am happy to finally meet you.*

Merridy lifted fingers he hadn't bothered to use to speak in weeks. He hadn't needed sign language around the band. *I'm happy to meet you too.*

Lugh smiled at him, a smile identical to the one Merridy saw every day in the mirror, and Merridy froze, a little shiver running through him. Holy crap. That really was his father! The man he'd always wanted to meet, who looked so much like him. The man whose music stirred up his own. *How did—? Where did—? My mom—* He didn't know what to ask first.

It was all so much—too much—swirling in his head. Merridy worried he might pass out again from the shock of it all, but he stayed completely aware and totally unsure of what he ought to do next.

"You will have to spend time together over the next few weeks. Lugh is the only one capable of teaching you to use your magic, so I expect there will be plenty of time for you both to ask all the questions that I have no doubt are on your minds—"

Someone knocked, interrupting Dian Cecht. Lugh opened the door, and a giant of a man ducked low to fit through the considerably smaller doorway. He was holding someone in his arms, Merridy noticed once he finished being distracted by seeing someone well over eight feet tall with the width to match his height.

Fion! Merridy gasped. He scrambled out from under the covers and to the edge of the bed, but was stopped from jumping off by Dian Cecht's outstretched hand. The giant set Fion on the bed with Merridy, and he was glad to see Fion didn't look any more hurt than before. He still wasn't breathing, but he didn't look dead.

"And now you see why Quinn's plan would never have worked," Dian Cecht said as he reached out and gently placed his hand on Fion's forehead. "One of my granddaughters is Fion's mother, and unlike Quinn, Fion does not have any Unseelie leanings hiding in his heart. He is purely his father's child, and he and I spoke before he embarked on his mission. I was able to gauge his personality enough to know he would never betray Underhill."

As Merridy listened to Dian Cecht speak, he saw Fion's chest start to rise and fall regularly. Merridy couldn't help letting out a breath of relief at the sight.

"Quinn was exiled because of his Unseelie heart, but also because he tries to use Underhill for his own benefit. If I hadn't acted, Underhill would have, and many more people would have died as a result. Although, given Underhill dropped you off right at Quinn's doorstep, I think Underhill was pushing me to take a second look." He sighed heavily and shook his head like a parent disappointed in their errant child.

"He's been put in a cell," the giant rumbled.

"Where he will stay until Underhill and I come to some sort of agreement on what to do with him," Dian Cecht concluded. "Your good work tonight is appreciated, Captain. You are dismissed."

"Yes, sir," the giant said before spinning on one heel and walking back out the door.

"Now, where was I before I was distracted? Ah, yes, training." Dian Cecht nodded to himself. "You will have to be properly trained in the use of your magic. The story you told my dining hall—while beautiful—was no doubt unintended. Throwing magic around so recklessly is draining, so after a full day without eating properly and being terribly stressed, the magic did as magic always does and took its due. That's why you fainted, I'm afraid."

Fion's breath suddenly caught in his chest, and his eyes flew open.

"Dian Cecht? Why am I with you?" He looked around the room from his prone position, taking in Lugh by the door before he looked the other way and saw Merridy. "Merry! You're okay. I was so worried!"

Quinn only threatened me, Merridy said soothingly, holding out his hands to press Fion back onto the bed when Fion tried to sit. *He wanted me to kill Dian Cecht in return for not killing you.*

"Obviously you figured out what to do," Fion replied, his grin wide and appreciative. "We need to get back Overhill to let the rest of the guys know we're alive and to see whether they made it. We were ambushed," he explained to Dian Cecht and Lugh, who were both looking curiously at Fion. "They were waiting outside our house for us to return."

"You both had the ambush in your minds as well as the need for a healer as you traversed Underhill?" Dian Cecht asked, his voice soft and thoughtful. He leaned back in his chair and looked up at the ceiling as he thought, then looked down at both of them. "I find it rather coincidental that Underhill would take both of those events and set you down on my errant grandson's doorstep. I believe we should have a talk with him. But not until the morning," he added quickly when Fion made to sit up again. "I will see a messenger is sent Overhill to your compatriots to ascertain their fate and to inform them of what has occurred to you. Both of you need rest after your ordeal. Take tonight, and in the morning we will move forward."

He stood and looked at both Merridy and Fion one more time before walking to the door.

"I will have food sent. The bathing facilities are through that door there. Take a hot bath, eat, and sleep. Things will be better in the morning." With those parting words, he walked out the door. Lugh smiled and awkwardly waved goodbye to Merridy before following. He shut the door behind him, leaving Merridy and Fion alone.

Chapter Eleven

Fion carefully pushed Merridy's hands away and sat up, but only scooted forward on the bed so he was next to Merridy.

"What really happened?" he asked gently, clasping one of Merridy's hands in one of his. His blue eyes were soft and full of worry.

Quinn put you in a coma and said he would kill you if I didn't kill Dian Cecht first, Merridy explained quickly, knowing his voice sounded bland and emotionless compared to how fraught the experience had actually been.

Fion shook his head slowly. "I'm so sorry, Merry. I'm sorry I trusted him and that I ended up putting you through that. I'm sorry," he repeated mournfully.

It's— Merridy had to swallow hard and take a deep breath to suppress suddenly budding tears before he could continue. *It's okay. I played the piano for Dian Cecht and for Lugh, and they sent someone to save you.*

"Still, I should have been there with you."

You saved my life by stopping that snake. You were hurt, and it was my turn to save you. I'm just glad you're safe.

They shared a smile, and Merridy bent forward to mirror Fion's own lean. Their lips met briefly in a chaste kiss. Fion pulled away, and they shared another smile before Fion bent forward again. This time their lips met with more intensity, and Merridy groaned at the sensation of wet heat stroking along his tongue and the safe pressure of Fion's hands pressed against his back, holding Merridy close. It was easily the best kiss he had ever had.

This time, when Fion drew away, his smile was a touch more carnal, but then he let out a wide yawn.

"Sorry, that wasn't sexy at all, was it?" he mumbled through the hand he had lifted to cover his mouth.

Merridy couldn't help laughing. He reached out and pulled Fion's hand down, then quickly leaned forward to peck Fion on the lips one more time.

We should shower before the food comes. Once we figure out the Fomoiri, we can try again?

"Maybe before we go after the Fomoiri? That might take a while, and I don't want to wait to spend time with you. But, yes, for right now, a shower and food sounds like a good idea. I don't know about you, but I might be too tired for anything more than kissing anyway." Fion laughed wryly. "Who would have thought I would be so tired after spending so long asleep?"

I'm tired, too, and I was sleeping an hour ago. I think it's Underhill. Merridy reluctantly slid off the side of the bed and headed to the bathroom door.

Inside, he was happy to see a set of towels and two pairs of sleeping pants already laid out next to the shower door. He stripped and jumped into the shower. He felt grimy from the sweat of the day, the two lengthy treks he had taken through Underhill, the fight beforehand, and even from playing the piano all day beforehand. It was wonderful to feel the layers of dirt and stress flow off his shoulders under the onslaught of excellent pressure from the hot water. Reluctantly he finally got out, and that was only because he knew Fion no doubt wanted a shower, too, and needed it more than he did. Still, the shower had served one important purpose: he had managed to calm his body after their wonderful kiss.

Merridy dried off and slipped into the waiting pajamas, knowing he could walk back into the bedroom without embarrassing himself or even jumping Fion like he really wanted to do.

"The food came," Fion said when Merridy walked back out of the bathroom. He had a bowl of something steaming in front of him where he was sitting at the table. He ignored the spoon and greedily brought the bowl up to his lips to gulp it down. "Sorry, I'm really starving." Merridy was starving too. He hurried over and found a second bowl full of some sort of meaty stew and what looked like a loaf of garlic bread.

It's safe to eat? Merridy had to ask, even as he was ripping off a piece of the bread. The butter got on his fingers immediately, and the aroma of garlic and tarragon had his mouth watering.

Fion barely had to say "yes" before Merridy had the entire slice stuffed in his mouth.

"Food in Underhill can be unpredictable. It's usually a safe bet that a red apple will be poisonous, but you can never be too careful with berries and nuts you find in the wild. The real problem with Underhill, though, is you never know who might be out to poison you. We're a rather bloodthirsty lot, and there's always some sort of grudge match going on, or a perceived slight. Poisons can also be weird here. Sometimes they just make you very ill, but sometimes they act like a magic spell instead. A good poison could turn you into someone's willing slave, for example."

Fion paused in his explanation to gulp down more stew and reached across the table for a slice of the bread to dip in the broth. Merridy was doing much the same with his own food—table manners be damned because he was so unbelievably hungry.

"Dian Cecht has a reputation as a prominent healer to uphold. It's usually a very safe assumption that eating his food is okay. Since I'm his grandson and Lir's son, and you're Lugh's son, there's no way he or anyone inside these walls would dare use food to hurt us," Fion continued. "Basically, as long as you know the food was prepared by allies who have no political reason to harm you, you're safe to eat here."

And don't go foraging in the woods for berries, Merridy finished with a grin.

Fion let out another wide, jaw-cracking yawn before he could return Merridy's smile. "I'm going to jump in the shower before I fall asleep right here. Finish eating and go to bed, Merry. Don't wait up for me." Merridy nodded and returned to his food while Fion slowly stood and wandered into the bathroom.

*

Merridy felt morning came far too soon. The sun shone brightly through the window and directly onto Merridy's face. As he rolled over to escape its glare, the ache in his legs from all of the walking the previous day made itself known. He tried to stretch under the covers and felt the pull of well-worked muscles as he pointed his toes.

The bed shifted next to him, and Merridy suddenly remembered that Fion was sharing with him. Merridy rolled the rest of the way over and saw Fion blinking blearily up at the canopy over their heads. He lifted one hand to rub at an eye while yawning widely.

"Why are we awake, Merry?" Fion grumbled as he rolled over to look at Merridy. "It's far too early."

Sorry, I didn't mean to wake you, Merridy replied contritely.

"Nah. Not your fault. I should have thought to close the curtains last night to keep the sun out. I know how insistent Underhill can be about things like this."

That made no sense to Merridy, but before he could ask, a knock sounded on the bedroom door.

Fion let out a groan as he rolled out of bed. He walked to the door to answer it, and Merridy got a very good look at his firm behind in his well-fitting pajama pants. That was definitely a sight Merridy could get used to in the morning. Fion looked over his shoulder at Merridy and winked, which meant he had probably heard Merridy's thoughts loud and clear.

Merridy's face heated up in embarrassment, but he got out of bed as a woman walked into the room carrying a tray that smelled absolutely delicious. She deposited the tray on the table and turned to Merridy and Fion.

"His Lordship says when you're dressed and ready, you should meet him in the great hall. He would like you with him when he goes to speak with the traitor." She bowed to them both before hurrying out of the room.

"I guess that means we don't have time for any fun this morning," Fion said as he closed the door behind her. He looked Merridy up and down, taking in Merridy's naked chest and the rest of him covered by pajamas, and grinned. "Too bad."

The blush that had been starting to fade on Merridy's face returned full force. *Definitely later then*, he replied firmly.

They fell on their breakfast ravenously and then hurried to get dressed. Sometime in the night, the clothing Merridy had left folded in the bathroom had been cleaned, so he felt fresh and ready for the new day by the time he and Fion left the bedroom and headed into the main hallways of the castle.

Fion knew where they were going, so Merridy let him lead the way through the sometimes twisting and turning halls. They all looked the same—built out of identical gray blocks of stone, each one easily bigger than Merridy's head. Only the occasional tapestry or side table showed they weren't walking in circles. Eventually they reached a staircase, which they walked down, through a massive set of doors at the bottom, and into the grand room where Merridy had played the piano for all the diners.

The room was empty at the moment, though the long tables were set and waiting for breakfast to be served. Dian Cecht stood from his seat at the table in the center of the dais and came to meet them at the door.

"There you are," he said. "Now, we know what Quinn was hoping to do with both of you, so we're going to use that as our in when we try to figure out why Underhill had to so forcefully bring him to my attention again. Let me and my captain do all the talking unless you hear something particularly important to you. Okay?" Dian Cecht looked at both of them searchingly, as if he needed to see their agreement, before he nodded to himself and turned to lead the way deeper into the castle.

They reached another staircase after about five minutes. This staircase was tight and dark, and they had to walk down one by one. Merridy placed a hand on the wall to help keep his balance. At the bottom of the stairs was exactly what Merridy had expected, given the dark and dank atmosphere: a dungeon. There were four cells, two on each side of the foot of the stairs. Three of the doors were open. Behind the fourth, Merridy could see Quinn lying indolently on a hard, wooden frame in the far corner. The giant from the night before was standing next to the door, his arms crossed over his broad chest and a heavy frown on his face.

"You have angered Underhill again, boy," Dian Cecht scolded as he reached the cell door.

"And?" Quinn replied with an indifferent shrug. He did sit up and turn toward Dian Cecht though.

"If you do not stop doing that, Underhill will either finally kill you and yours, or Underhill will label you Unseelie and shove you across their dark doorstep. I do not want that for you—or for any of my family."

Quinn sneered at him. "What do you care? I'm just another one of your brats. You've got so many to spare; you can afford to lose me."

Dian Cecht was very, very quiet for a few minutes. It was the kind of silence that weighed down everyone in the room, and Merridy wouldn't have dared break it, even if Dian Cecht hadn't already warned him not to speak.

"I feel that you actually, truly believe that, which means I have failed you, Quinn." When he said Quinn's name, Merridy's ears heard the usual five-letter name, but somehow it sounded like four or five syllables. "I am a healer of bodies and souls, yet I never noticed your pain." Dian Cecht's voice was shaking with grief, the emotion so strong tears choked the back of Merridy's throat. Merridy swallowed hard and tried to stay focused. They needed to know what Quinn had done to anger Underhill in the first place. Still, he couldn't interrupt Dian Cecht.

Quinn had looked down at his hands, as if—like Merridy—he was having trouble listening to the anguish in what Dian Cecht was saying.

"How can I fix this?" Dian Cecht continued. "All of my strongest magics cannot heal the rift between us, nor the pain in your heart, unless you tell me what it is you have done so we can begin to fix the mess."

Quinn shook his head, but not as if he were saying no to Dian Cecht. It was more like he was trying to say no to some sort of internal thought.

"I don't know who they are, not really," Quinn said softly. He didn't seem to be able to raise his voice any louder. "Just that they're tired of the status quo. They don't think Nuada should be high king, or that you should have so much power as his second. I don't think they want to go back to Lir and Lugh either. It's like they want exactly the opposite of what Underhill decreed, yet they can't say for certain what that is, only that they're angry they don't have it. I was angry too—I still am angry—but for a different reason. They pulled on that part of me and convinced me that by helping them I would also help free myself from the situation you stuck me in. I was given a simple enough task: should any of Lir's children be injured and forced to return to Underhill for healing, I was to coerce Underhill to send them to me. How was I to know that Underhill had already seen through their plan and was using me to get you to act instead?"

"They knew Lir's children had gone Overhill?" Dian Cecht asked sharply. "The only ones who were supposed to know that were Nuada's council."

"They didn't hear it from the council," Quinn replied just as sharply, a contemptuous sneer twisting his lips.

"They knew if they sent the Fomoiri Overhill, Nuada would have to act. He couldn't send Lugh or Lir again, not when they hadn't aged and the human world might recognize them and be curious. A new group would have to go in their stead. Who better than Lir's children? Strong, young Sidhe eager to prove themselves after that debacle with the swans, who were looking for some direction in life, and were eager for any assignment. It was supposed to be a trap. Use the Fomoiri to draw out Lir's children, then kill them off to weaken Lir and to ultimately prove to Underhill that Nuada is unfit to rule. Something must have gone right in their plan, since these two were forced here," he finished with a nod to Merridy and Fion.

Dian Cecht immediately turned to them. "Go. Make certain the rest of Lir's children still live. Captain?" he added to the giant, who had been silent so far.

"I will summon what troops I have capable of crossing to Overhill. The Fomoiri won't stand a chance." He grinned, and his big, square teeth were somehow more ominous-looking than if had they been pointed like a shark's. The giant nodded politely to Dian Cecht and then hurried past them and up the stairs. Fion reached out to grip Merridy's hand and pulled Merridy up the stairs too.

"We need a fresh breeze full of Underhill's gentle touch," he explained as he jogged through the halls. "Put the thought of our mansion back Overhill into the front of your mind, and Underhill will read our intent and let us leave."

It took a few minutes to traverse the halls, but as they burst through the front doors at a run, Merridy did as Fion had said and thought of the mansion. The music rooms where he and the band had worked so hard to write their songs and to practice until they had the notes perfected. The weapons practice room, a place Merridy so badly wanted to hate, but couldn't help enjoying at the same time. All the halls and the rooms, and even the expansive lawn, were completely familiar to him after so many weeks living there among his friends.

Underhill wavered around him, and suddenly he was running up to the front door of the mansion. He and Fion skidded to a stop, and Fion reached out to open the door.

"Hello?" Fion called as they stepped inside.

It was eerily silent for a long moment, during which Merridy's worst fears started to creep up on him. Had the rest of the band made it off the side of the road that night? What if they had gone into the woods after Merridy and Fion and had gotten caught in the same trap? But then Merridy heard the slap of running footsteps, and Conn skidded into view from the direction of the kitchen.

"You're okay!" Conn gasped, dashing forward to pull them both into a hug. "We were so worried, but Raven insisted you had gone Underhill, and then the messenger arrived late last night saying you had ended up at Dian Cecht's place!"

"We've got a huge problem," Fion said, cutting into Conn's excitement. "Where is everyone else?"

"We were having a late lunch. Come eat and tell us what you know." Conn waved toward the kitchen and then followed his own gesture, leading the way.

Raven, Aed, and Rylee all jumped to their feet when Merridy and Fion walked into the kitchen. Merridy didn't think Aed had ever shown him any sort of affection before—he had always been so impatiently waiting for the battle to start, and now that it was over, apparently, he could give his focus to something else—so the hug he pulled Merridy into was a touch startling.

Rylee pulled two more plates out of the cabinet and put a premade sandwich down on each. Merridy and Fion took seats around the table, and Merridy was happy to have food in front of him. Underhill had really exhausted him, because he was starving again.

"This was a trap from the start," Fion began seriously. He hadn't picked up his sandwich yet, and his eyes were very serious. "They knew if they sent the Fomoiri Overhill, Lir and Nuada would specifically send us to investigate. Killing us in the trap would weaken Nuada's position Underhill and could throw the leadership into disarray, which would allow whoever planned this to maybe take power instead."

"That's a plot right out of the most twisted Unseelie mind," Raven said. A deep frown filled his face, which was echoed by Conn's disgusted snort.

"I feel it's safe to assume we're surrounded," Rylee added. "We need to all get out of here and safely back Underhill. Once the enemy realizes we beat their plan and got away safely, they should pull the Fomoiri back. Unfortunately, the closest circle that will get us back Underhill is in the woods, where the Fomoiri are no doubt waiting for us."

"So we have to fight our way free," Aed replied, a touch more eagerly than Merridy felt was actually warranted. Couldn't they just stay safe in the mansion until the Fomoiri got bored and left?

Fion grinned at him, and then turned a more serious face to Aed. "Dian Cecht is sending reinforcements. They should be here soon, and together we'll set up a plan to take out the Fomoiri and get to safety."

Conn shook his head. "By the time they get here, it'll be dark. That gives the Fomoiri an advantage, which sounds like a bad idea to me."

"We won't be able to find the Fomoiri in the daylight anyway," Rylee cut in before the argument could escalate. "They'll be buried in their hidey-holes until the sun sets."

Why don't we escape now instead? Merridy asked. If the goal was to get back to Underhill where it was safe, couldn't they just run to a mushroom circle while the Fomoiri were sleeping?

Even Fion was shaking his head in response to Merridy's question.

"We're Sidhe who have been assigned the duty of ridding Overhill of the Fomoiri scourge. If we don't return victorious in battle, we will be sent back anyway. It's better to make a stand now, when we know where they are."

Fion's explanation did make some sense, but Merridy couldn't help wondering how much of Fion's words were fueled by the lust for blood and battle.

Fion glanced sidelong at Merridy, and his shrug was slightly sheepish, but he didn't say anything else, so Merridy knew the answer didn't matter. They would be fighting in the woods tonight.

"Rest up until reinforcements arrive," Rylee finished. "We'll regroup in a few hours."

Merridy took the last few bites of his sandwich and left the kitchen. He wanted a shower and some time on the piano to relax before everything he knew he would have to endure that night.

Chapter Twelve

The forest was actually a rather lovely place. Birds were chirping their bedtime songs as they settled into their nests for the night, and the first of the nighttime bugs and frogs had started their own songs. The dissonance between the two different styles was pleasant to Merridy's ear. It was dark under the spread orange and yellow leaves of the trees even though the barest sliver of sunlight was supposed to still be visible on the horizon.

The Fomoiri would appear at any moment, and then the battle would begin.

Merridy had a quiverful of small throwing spears hanging at his hip. Leaning against the tree next to him were five longer spears for thrusting and defense. He held a sixth in his hands.

Fion was standing at his back, his sword in his hands and knives strapped to his hips, arms, and legs. The entire forest surrounding the mansion was filled with fighting pairs. Dian Cecht had sent over thirty men and women, all of whom had also paired off and scattered to strategic positions. The forest was too dense to try fighting together as one army.

Merridy knew there were three mushroom circles within easy distance of his position should he and Fion get overrun, but Conn and Rylee were just one copse of trees over, so backup was nearby too.

And all Merridy wanted was to be back in the mansion, plucking away at the piano.

He felt a little bit like he had been coerced into this. He wasn't a fighter, and had only signed up to play music with the band. Yet the spear in his hands still called to him as fervently as ever. He also couldn't leave Fion alone in the woods, not when he could be there to ensure Fion's back was protected.

So, yes, Merridy didn't want to be standing in the woods waiting for the bloodshed to begin, but he also knew he wouldn't be able to stand sitting at home waiting. He had to help.

"Ready, Merry?" Fion said softly. He didn't turn away from his position, but Merridy could feel Fion's concern in the air, as tangible as the gentle breeze rustling the leaves overhead.

If I have to be, Merridy replied.

"Good. They're coming." Fion lifted his sword into position and let out a heavy breath.

Merridy could hear them too. The ground-rattling footsteps of massive creatures, the slither of snakes, and the slug rustle of creatures like the very first one Merridy had killed were slowly coming closer. The grunting, yells, and crash of metal against bone reached him next as neighboring pairs were swept into the fight. Merridy gripped the spear in his hand tighter and squinted into the dark, trying to see the slightest movement.

There! Something with blotchy orange skin, four arms, and a long tail slithered into view. Action came before thought, and a throwing spear was flung from his hand before he had consciously decided to attack. The metal point hit dead center in the creature's chest, and it let out a screech as it fell back, black ash already crumbling away from the cold steel as it fell to the ground and stopped moving.

Feeling sad about it was the last conscious thought Merridy had before his world filled with the screaming of creatures and the all-encompassing lure of the battle. He threw spear after spear. They came to his hand from the quiver as if called by magic—and maybe they were. When the Fomoiri grew too close for throwing, Merridy gripped his first long spear and thrust, knowing if he faltered here, the wickedly long claws of the green swamp monster he was fighting would end up in Fion's back. Merridy fought and fought and let the fight take him away.

Even here, in the middle of a forest filled with unimaginable creatures and the screams of battle, there was music. He heard the beat first, a pounding *thump-thump* that he quickly realized was his heart. Then the metallic crash of weapons clashing like cymbals. Even the screaming had a strange sort of harmony to it, and the discord as the death yells fought against the cries of triumph added to a cacophony of sound. Fion's song about fighting immediately jumped to the front of Merridy's mind, the notes and beat of the song slotting easily into the sounds of battle.

> *The battle, the fight, so eager for blood,*
>
> *The kill, the triumph, the will to stand tall,*
>
> *Of bodies and screams, you hear none of their cries.*

Of pain, and of death, look at the soaked ground you stand on.

Oblivious,

Your heart calls for conflict, never realizing those you hurt as you strive.

Oblivious,

Your soul dreams of the next mountain, not remembering those you left behind.

Oblivious.

There were so many Fomoirians in the woods. Merridy could feel his arm tiring. It took a second longer to find a new spear in his quiver now, as if the magic of battle that strengthened his grip was beginning to wane. Next to him, Fion was panting for breath. Merridy took a half second to look over and saw Fion's sword flash just a beat too slow. The creature he was battling had three pairs of arms, and all six hands held blades. Fion blocked one slash, turned his sword to knock back another, and just barely got it back around to block a third.

Merridy had to focus on his side of the clearing again as something with whiplike tentacle limbs ran at him. He threw a spear and watched the creature's purple skin immediately turn gray and start to flake off when it connected.

He and Fion weren't alone in their exhaustion setting in. The Fomoirian army felt endless. The air had a heavy atmosphere due to the desperation from everyone around them beginning to permeate, as if the forest had taken on a minor tone full of the belief that defeat was inevitable.

They needed help, or at least something or someone to motivate them into a second wind, but no one else was coming. That meant someone already here had to do something. But what?

The beat continued to throb in the air, but it was slowing. Merridy had to do something before it faded entirely. But what? There wasn't anything more he could do with his spear than he was already doing, and it wasn't as if there was a piano or guitar handy.

But there was music in the air that only he could hear. He took a deep breath, opened his mouth, and sang.

No sound came out of his mouth, of course, but a wind immediately rustled through the trees. It stirred the air, blowing the heavy minor chords through the blanket of leaves across the ground. It lightened the sound, echoing sharply as if there were wind chimes hanging from the branches overhead. Merridy took that light feeling in with his breathing and let it back out as song.

> *The battle, the fight, a mindless refrain,*
>
> *The kill, the triumph, glory in each thrust,*
>
> *Of clashing and steel, you see none of their blood.*
>
> *Of mercy, and of love, you feel no concern for the slain.*

> *Oblivious,*
>
> *Your heart calls for conflict, never realizing those you hurt as you strive*
>
> *Oblivious,*
>
> *Your soul dreams of the next mountain, not remembering those you left behind*
>
> *Oblivious.*

It was working. Fion's breathing was evening, and the six-armed creature let out a death scream as Fion took care of him. Merridy sensed renewed hope in the air, and the knowledge that the enemy wasn't endless. It was a complete change, but Merridy could feel the negative dissonance just waiting to reassert itself. He had to keep singing, and to keep fighting. A spear came to his hand even as he switched to another song and fell back into the rhythms of the forest.

There was no telling how much more time had passed, but Merridy's arms burned and his throat was sore from the magic. He was panting for breath, and sweat was dripping off his forehead. No practice session with Conn had ever felt this brutal. At the same time, he didn't think any practice session could ever compare to the horror of the real thing. How was it possible to practice hearing the pained cries of those Merridy had just killed, or to practice feeling that awful give as flesh parted under the pointed blade of his spear?

"Pick up your spears before another wave comes through. I'll watch your back," Fion said. He didn't sound tired in the least, but he was far more practiced at something like this than Merridy. Merridy hated Fion for that fact for a brief moment, but he pushed it aside easily. This was the life Fion had lived, thanks to growing up in Underhill. It was a world Merridy was now part of, and while Merridy never wanted to have to go into battle again, it was a part of him now. Separating the spear from his hand would no doubt be as difficult as keeping him away from a piano. And that was another sad thought, so Merridy also pushed it away. It would come back to haunt him later—of that he had zero doubts—but now wasn't the time for tears.

He obeyed Fion, carefully walking around the clearing to retrieve the spears he had thrown and dropping them back into his quiver for later. One of his long spears was cracked down the middle, so he left it. He tried not to look at what was left of the creatures, but the blackened, burnt flesh would be stuck in his memory forever. He did manage not to count how many he had killed, which was only a slight relief.

Fion's side of the clearing was bloodier, but he looked okay to Merridy as he handed over a water bottle when Merridy rejoined him. Merridy drank greedily, then handed it back.

How many more do you think there are? he asked Fion, trying not to hope that this terrible night had finally come to an end.

Fion's responding grimace was as gentle as the fingers he used to brush hair off Merridy's damp forehead.

"We have to stay until the retreat is sounded," he replied. "But listen. I don't hear much more fighting going on around us either." He went silent for a few moments to let Merridy listen, and he was right; the sounds of battle had quieted around them. "You okay over there?" Fion called in a louder voice in the direction Conn and Rylee had been stationed.

"Rylee's going to have another nice scar to show off to his lady friends, but otherwise we're fine," Conn yelled back. He also didn't sound winded, while Merridy was just starting to catch his breath. "How are you two?"

"Not a scratch on us," Fion replied smugly.

"Hah," Conn snorted, but whatever else he was going to add was lost as the sound of horns blowing filled the forest.

It was a joyous sound, uplifting in tone as it rose in scale. It had to be a victory cry, and Fion's wide grin confirmed that for Merridy.

"To Underhill?" Conn called.

"See you there!" Fion grabbed Merridy's hand and led the way toward the nearest mushroom circle. They both stepped inside, and the bloody forest wavered around them for a moment before the bright sunlight of Underhill and the front gate of Dian Cecht's castle quickly replaced it.

One by one, pairs of fighters joined them as other people began to rush out of the gates. Merridy saw a number of injured fighters get placed onto litters and carried inside—no doubt to where Dian Cecht and his family of healers would take care of them. Conn and Rylee joined them a few moments later. Conn was grinning ear to ear, and Rylee looked pleased despite the bleeding gash in his right arm. Aed and Raven were next to find them, and Merridy couldn't help letting out a sigh of relief to see that all of his friends were safe.

"Let's go get healed up," Rylee said. "Take a bath, change our clothes, and rejuvenate ourselves and such. I'm sure there will be a grand banquet in our honor tonight!" He turned without waiting for them to agree and headed into the castle, hopefully straight to someone who could take a look at his arm.

"Not a bad idea," Conn added. He scratched at a bit of dried, purple blood staining one of his cheeks. Then he looked at Merridy, and his eyes were sharp and knowing. "Don't go to sleep before the banquet—you'll only have nightmares. You handled yourself well during the fight, so go take a bath and let yourself cry. Then let yourself be held by Fion. Let go of all the pain and sorrow in your heart. Be joyous with us tonight as we celebrate our triumph, and then tomorrow we will really begin the long healing all our souls will need."

Fion was still holding Merridy's hand, and that warmth, combined with Conn's understanding of what was going through his mind, lifted some of the weight holding a spear caused. He was with someone he could love, surrounded by friends who understood him.

Merridy couldn't do anything else but smile at them. *Then we should party tonight.*

Epilogue

Wine was flowing as quickly as servants could bring it out. Platters of food strained the tables, and even as one platter was emptied, another full one replaced it. The noise in the room was intense, a cacophony of hundreds of voices laughing and talking all at the same time. A portion of the noise wasn't audible to a regular ear. Merridy wasn't the only one in the room who could speak without words. Just as many thoughts were flying around the room as words, and while Merridy wasn't as proficient at hearing as he was speaking, it was causing a background buzz in his head.

Of course, all the wine he had drunk could also cause that buzz.

Everyone was so incredibly happy. It was like Conn had said: celebrate tonight; mourn for the toll the battle had taken tomorrow. It was hard though. Every time Merridy closed his eyes, an image of one of the creatures he had skewered flashed across his mind, and then the accompanying dying scream of agony filled his ears. He took gulp of wine every time that happened, hoping the alcohol would help dull the memories. It wasn't working— and Merridy didn't know why he had expected it to—but it did explain why the room continued to get more and more boisterous and why so much wine was flowing in the first place.

Merridy was sitting on the dais. Dian Cecht was holding court in the center of the table, and Aed, Conn, Raven, and Rylee were sitting to his right. Lugh was on his left, with Merridy sitting on Lugh's other side. Fion was, of course, sitting next to Merridy too. Their arms kept brushing, and every time Merridy looked over at Fion, his thoughts drifted where the wine willed until he found himself blushing and looking away. Fion, who no doubt was still reading Merridy's mind, only grinned happily at him. In that grin, Merridy saw the promise of a bed and them trying out those naughty thoughts. Just...not while Lugh would want to know why Merridy was sneaking out of the party early.

Lugh seemed to be happy just sitting next to Merridy. He had always been a man of few words, according to the television interviews Merridy had watched. Merridy had simply assumed that was because he couldn't talk, but Lugh could sign and speak with Merridy just fine.

It was honestly kind of nice, and Merridy could totally understand how Lugh and his mother had managed to spend so much time together. His mother liked to talk, sometimes to the point that Merridy couldn't take it anymore. He didn't think Lugh would ever get impatient with her.

"Bard!" someone sitting off the dais yelled over the noise. "Bard, play for us!"

"Yes, play!" another voice called.

Then the rest of the room caught on, and suddenly the chants of "play, play, play" filled the room.

Merridy looked up at Lugh, expecting him to stand and find an instrument. A couple of servants were already rolling the piano kept at the other end of the room up to the dais. Lugh smiled at Merridy and lifted his fingers to sign.

"I would like to hear you play again," Lugh signed.

Fion? Want to play with me? Merridy asked, turning toward Fion with a hopeful smile.

Fion stood, and the room fell silent. "Someone get me a guitar."

Conn let out a happy laugh and stood as well. "And a drum!"

Aed and Raven were also laughing as they stood and walked around the long table to the short staircase that led down to the main floor and the waiting piano. Merridy was the last to get to his feet, but his heart was light with joy as he joined his band.

Two guitars were located, and a little hand drum. Merridy sat at the piano, and Aed stepped up in front of them all, humming slightly to himself to warm up his voice. They didn't even have to talk about which song they would sing. Merridy hit a chord on the piano to give the singers their starting notes, Conn set the tempo with his fingers tapping along the drum, and then Aed started singing.

> *In my dreams, I know you see me.*
> *And in my hopes, you'll hold my hand.*
> *Reality hits, so does the truth:*
> *You and me will never be we.*
>
> *Another dream, a hand on my shoulder,*
> *Someone smiling only at me.*

You're laughing, so happy.
Reality hits, and I'm still alone.

If a butterfly don't fly, it falls.
You are my wings; you are my wings,
Broken wings, shattered, torn.
You are my wings, and I'm falling hard.

Dinner at five; party's at six.
Across the room, I see your smile.
You're not looking at me.
You haven't, not for a while.

Broken heart, the tears I've cried,
I'm done with all your lies.
Oh, yes, I'm done with your damn lies.

If a butterfly don't fly, it falls.
You are my wings; you are my wings,
Broken wings, shattered, torn.
You are my wings, and I'm breaking free.

Flying without wings, I should fail.
The ground should near; pain should invade.
A hand on my shoulder; it's not a dream.
Who's watching me, as I once watched you?

Hope in my heart, you're with me.
Can I hold your hand? Please don't leave.
Reality hits; you're still here.
You and me will always be we.

If a butterfly don't fly, it falls.
You are my wings; you are my wings,
Broken wings, shattered, torn.
My wings can soar, and I'm flying high.

Fion was the one looking at Merridy as the song came to a close, and the longing in his eyes suddenly told Merridy just what had inspired the lyrics in this song. They rang true to Merridy's own experiences with love, but Fion had loved and lost as well. That pain, combined with the hope for a new love in the future, had definitely inspired him.

Except Fion's eyes were saying the last line had come true for him. He was soaring high thanks to Merridy having given him back his wings.

The feelings Fion evoked were amazing, and Merridy wanted more than ever to escape to their bedroom, where he could let Fion know just how much he appreciated that trust. That would still have to wait until later, however, as the band smoothly transitioned to another song.

They played "Mating Call," and then the jig about Underhill that had the entire room singing along. People were banging in time on the tables, and for the faster songs, some were even dancing.

Merridy took it all in as his fingers flew across the piano keys. This was his ultimate dream, the one he had imagined during those long hours plodding through the Bard and Sons building while wearing his ill-fitting security guard uniform. Playing the instrument he loved, surrounded by friends playing music in their own particular ways, in front of a lively and engaged audience... It was practically magic. He didn't want it to ever end, but the band only had so many songs under their belt.

When Changeling's Court finally stepped aside, someone else was ready to eagerly step up to take their place. Fueled by drink and good food, it didn't matter to anyone in the room whether they were as good as the band, just that they all had fun with it. Merridy found his fingers tapping along with some of the songs as he sat through dessert.

When the dessert dishes were cleared, Dian Cecht stood and looked to either side of the table. "Shall we adjourn to more pleasant quarters?" he asked them all. Merridy didn't know if he meant he wanted to go to bed, or just wanted to leave the ever more boisterous hall, but Merridy was more than happy to stand and join Dian Cecht and the rest of the dais in leaving the hall out of a side door.

Dian Cecht didn't take them far, only down two twisting hallways until they reached a large sitting room. Merridy settled into a loveseat with Fion as everyone else found their own spots to sit. Dian Cecht went to a side table and started pouring drinks. It turned out to be some sort of whiskey, Merridy learned after taking a sip from one of the glasses.

"Settle a curiosity for me, if you all will," Dian Cecht said once he had relaxed into an armchair near the side table. "I would like to know what all of your plans are now that the Fomoiri army has been vanquished. I admit I could use individuals with your talents here in my court."

That was one of the things Merridy had been avoiding thinking about. Fion, Conn, Raven, and Aed had only come Overhill because of the Fomoiri, and now that it was all over, the band had no reason to remain. Merridy, on the other hand, still wanted to pursue his dream. Yet at the same time, he wanted to stay with Fion and with his friends. If they decided to stay Underhill, Merridy might have to stay too. He couldn't go back to being a security guard working a shitty shift.

When nobody answered for a long moment, Rylee spoke up. "I still have five more years on my contract as a sentinel. I'll be returning Overhill tomorrow to work on cleaning up the woods and resetting all the protections and alerts against attack. We may have won this battle, but the ones that sent the Fomoiri Overhill could try again. I will prepare for such an eventuality."

"I understand," Dian Cecht replied with a nod. "You are right that the larger players in this war are still active. We have dealt them a decisive loss, but I expect them to return in due time. Your work as a sentinel is much appreciated; however, if you are looking for a position once your tenure Overhill is completed, feel free to approach me. What about you five?"

I wouldn't mind spending more time with Merry, Lugh said. *It would be nice to get to know you properly.*

Merridy had to admit that was something he wanted, too, but that was just one more thing that was pulling him in a dozen different directions. Even if it meant more terrible battles in the future, he needed to know what Fion was doing to be able to make a proper decision. Merridy looked up at Fion curiously, knowing Fion had heard every single one of his thoughts on the matter.

Fion nodded at him, but turned to the rest of the band. "We were kind of awesome just now, playing like that."

"We were," Conn agreed immediately, "although I could have used a better drum."

"You should hear the second stanza Merry wrote to 'Oblivious,'" Fion continued. "It's amazing."

I barely changed your lyrics. It's not that impressive. Merridy gently elbowed Fion to get him to stop boasting about him. Fion just grinned cheekily.

"Oh, fine," Aed said with a grumble under his breath. "Fion, just come out and say it next time instead of this backhanded wheeling and dealing. You want all of us to go back Overhill with Rylee so Merridy can live out his dream of playing in a hit band. It's why he agreed to join us, after all. What's five years Overhill in return for Merridy's sacrifice? I'm in."

"Me too," Conn added immediately.

They both turned to look at Raven, who nodded. "I can't abandon my brothers now," he said softly. "Five years playing music while helping Rylee defend the world from the evils the Unseelie send his way doesn't sound too bad."

"That's our answer then," Fion said to Dian Cecht.

Lugh let out a heavy, disappointed sigh.

I'll visit, Merridy told him.

"We'll all visit," Conn said. "I'm not letting Lir think he's gotten rid of us this easily."

Five years to the Seelie is nothing, Lugh told Merridy. *Not when we can live to five thousand before feeling even the first effects of age. You will visit, and after five years are over, perhaps you will choose to live Underhill, perhaps not, but certainly you will have even more free time to spend with me. I do have to teach you to use your magic, remember.*

"Which he has to learn before he accidentally beguiles an entire stadium of humans." Rylee chuckled to himself. "I'll make sure he has time in his schedule to come Underhill for training. We'll have to get to work on the album when we get back, if you're going to be superstars inside five years."

Merridy grinned at them all. The rest of the band and even Lugh smiled back. Merridy leaned back in the loveseat, letting Fion's shoulder take his weight. Fion wrapped an arm around him in response.

"Good, that is decided," Dian Cecht said. "I will have to arrange for you all to come Underhill for a full performance. Rooms have been prepared for you tonight. Please join me for breakfast before you head out."

"We appreciate the hospitality," Rylee replied. "Let's enjoy the good whiskey and the good company, because once we get Overhill, I'm going to put you to work."

Merridy couldn't wait.

*

Six Months Later

"Changeling's Court, you're having something of a conundrum. You released two singles four months ago, and since then, both songs have been one-two on the charts. They've switched places at least four times that I'm aware of. I have to ask, which song do you want to be first?"

The interviewer flashed them a bright smile from where he was sitting behind his desk. The band was arrayed on a long couch at an angle where the television cameras could get them all into one shot without blocking too much of the live audience's view.

"I've been partial to 'Mating Call' since I wrote it," Aed answered. "I was feeling depressed over a recent breakup and was able to expunge a lot of emotion by putting it all down in lyrics."

"I like the drum line in 'Oblivious' best," Conn cut in when it looked like Aed was about to get mushy. "I know that's not one of the two singles, but it will definitely always be my favorite."

"'Oblivious' is absolutely a great song, and I know plenty of our viewers at home will agree with you there, Conn. What about you, Merridy?" the interviewer asked.

Merridy signed for the benefit of the human audience, but it was Fion's voice translating the words in his thoughts that answered. "Definitely 'If A Butterfly Don't Fly'." That earned a few chuckles from the audience, who by now had no doubt heard the often-repeated tale of how Merridy had helped write the song secretly by dropping scraps of notes onto the band's writing desk. "I'm soaring amazingly high on the wings being in this band has given me. I'm honored to be working with these wonderful guys, and I'm even more honored that you all continue to like our music."

"Both really are beautiful songs," the interviewer replied. "We're going to break for commercial now, but when we return, Changeling's Court will be playing 'If A Butterfly Don't Fly' for us. Don't change the channel!"

The band got up from the long couch and headed across the studio to where their instruments were waiting.

Merridy settled into his spot behind the keyboard and waited while the rest of the band fiddled with drumsticks, guitar straps, and the microphone stands. When everything was ready, the interviewer stepped in front of the cameras again.

"And now, playing their hit single 'If A Butterfly Don't Fly,' Changeling's Court!"

Merridy's fingers stroked along the plastic of the piano keys, pressing down to provide his harmonies to the guitar and Aed's singing, and he couldn't help closing his eyes to take in the utter bliss of the moment.

He had somehow learned to enjoy holding and practicing with a spear—although he would never enjoy actually fighting with it. He still loved playing music of all kinds, particularly with the band members who had become his brothers.

However, the best part was definitely playing with Fion, who would glance over at him periodically throughout the song and who inspired Merridy to play at his very best.

Putting love into his music for the sake of the music was wonderful, but putting love into his music for the man he loved was even better. Merridy couldn't be happier.

> *If a butterfly don't fly, it falls.*
> *You are my wings; you are my wings,*
> *Broken wings, shattered, torn.*
> *My wings can soar, and I'm flying high.*

About the Author

When Mell Eight was in high school, she discovered dragons. Beautiful, wondrous creatures that took her on epic adventures both to faraway lands and on journeys of the heart. Mell wanted to create dragons of her own, so she put pen to paper. Mell Eight is now known for her own soaring dragons, as well as for other wonderful characters dancing across the pages of her books. While she mostly writes paranormal or fantasy stories, she has been seen exploring the real world once or twice.

Facebook
www.facebook.com/MellEightFiction

Twitter
@MellEight

Website
www.melleightfiction.weebly.com

Other NineStar books by this author

Ge-Mi, Part One

Ge-Mi, Part Two

A Little Fairy Dust

Supernatural Consultant Series

Dragon Consultant

Dragon Deception
Dragon Dilemma
Dragon Detective
Dragon Soldier
Dragon Adventures
Dragon Lesson

Out of Underhill Series
Kelpie Blue

Magnified Series
Magnified
Justified

Also Available from NineStar Press

Connect with NineStar Press

www.ninestarpress.com

www.facebook.com/ninestarpress

www.facebook.com/groups/NineStarNiche

www.twitter.com/ninestarpress